mere observations

*Collections
of
interactive verse,
lyric poetry,
didactic prose,
narrative
and
descriptive
scenes.*

Copyright © 2002 Derek Garson

No part of this work covered by the copyrights hereon may be reproduced or used in any form or by any means - graphic, electronic, or mechanical - without prior written permission of the publisher Pemmican Publications Inc. Any requests for photocopying, recording, taping of information storage and retrieval systems of any part of this book shall be directed in writing to the Canadian Copyright Licensing Agency, 6 Adelaide Street East, Suite 900, Toronto, ON M5C 1H6.

Pemmican Publications Inc. gratefully acknowledges the assistance accorded to it's publishing program by the Manitoba Arts Council, Canada Arts Council and the Book Publishing Industry Development Program.

Printed and Bound in Canada

Book design by Sherry M. McPherson and Alicia Clarke

National Library of Canada Cataloguing in Publications Data

Garson, Derek, 1972-
    Mere observations

Poems.
ISBN 1-894717-11-2

I. Title.
PS8563.A6744M47 2002   jC811'.6   C2002-910774-1
PR9199.4.G37M47 2002

Ψ | mere observations

Contents

2   What is a mere observation?

3   COLLECTION ONE
    Sir Esse Ens of Esprit de Corps

53 COLLECTION TWO
    Sir Dreadlee Groove Esq.

87 COLLECTION THREE
    EupheMystic

107 COLLECTION FOUR
    Dovetale of Dei Versatile Ink

153 COLLECTION FIVE
    StrataGem's Pearl of Wisdom

Ψ

What is a mere observation?

Mere is a mispronunciation of the word mirror: "As I looked into the mere."
Observation is the objective reflection of one's self when one is
soul searching.

Mirror... of the S.O.U.L.
(The **S**pirit **O**f **U**nconditional **L**ife New and Love True)

Interactive Poetry* (Φ) is a dialogue between the unity of thought and feeling
where the consummation of the two are expressed in all that is
Word and Deed. The conclusion of the Thesis and the Antithesis of both
conception and perception is truly manifested within and throughout the
Synthesis of all that is **Said and Done**. Thus, **Mere Observations** is the sum
total of existence brought into a Contextual One.

En Theos: The Spirit (pneuma), the Soul (psyche), the Body (soma) and
their psycho-physical connection are explored as unified reality.
Life New becomes the intensity of these qualities perpetually redeemed.
Love True becomes the immensity of these quantities continually esteemed.

Ψ is the Psi symbol of the Greek alphabet.
It is also the symbol for modern day psychology.
Psychology = Psi (of psyche meaning soul) and Logos (meaning discourse).

$$\alpha \quad \text{first}$$

$$\Psi$$

$$\Omega \quad \text{last}$$

*For the Interactive poems (Φ) each line is written, read, and spoken with
another line back and forth. First and last parts of each section are separated by
the alpha (α) and omega (Ω) symbol. Some narrative and dramatic scenes
(mini-play) are of this interchangeable nature, not all. A mini-play is a
pictured scene where:
a) a character is entered via location or prologue;
b) a soliloquy and its oration is performed;
c) a character is exited via location or epilogue.

Ψ | mere observations

COLLECTION ONE
Sir Esse Ens of Esprit de Corps

2 Olive U

4 Olive U

Above and Beyond*

Above and Beyond II

Acknowledgement

Amidst Treachery

Butterfly Kisses*

Diamond Tear Drops*

Enslaved to Freedom

Equiponderance*

Frankincense and Myrrh

From Alpha to Omega*

From Cause to Effect: A Priori

Grand Expectation*

Great Ambition*

In Order - Numpa Echaga

In the Wake of Nature

Je Ne Sais Quoi

L.O.Y.A.L.

Mere Thought and Feeling

Meta 4 U

Music

14UNI2C

Once Twice

...of the Spirit

Nocturne

Orchestration of the Constellations*

Praecaedere

Psi Quotiens

Relative Relation*

Reunion

Spectrum*

Stepping Stones Skipping Upon the Rippling Waters of Time and Space*

That Which Is, Thereof

The Companion of Loneliness

The Dolphin and the Eagle Aforementioned

The Everlasting To Be

The Oracle of Sir Esse Ens

The Risen Son vs The Fallen One

The Truth - Word and Deed

The Union of Wisdom and Knowledge*

The Valley of the Shadow of Death

Thoughts Become*

Thoughts Become - The Reprise*

To Sense - Pennies from Heaven

To You for You

Unprecedented

Welcome

When Again

Interactive Poem

3

2 Olive U

A night without you
is like a day with no light;
many emotions so blue
that my eyes wish for prophetic sight.

Hours tick motionlessly by
as I do patiently wait for the 'all of you'.
For while my very heart unaware only does sigh,
it is Here that the wondering concern of my every part esteemed
breathes a breath which dreams of Where the reality of your love could be so true.

A day without you
is like the never ending night;
plenty devotions so few
that my ears wish to hear what is right.

Minutes pass motionlessly by
as I do silently contemplate 'all of you'.
For while my very soul solitaire lonely does cry,
it is Now that the wandering sojourn of my every goal redeemed
dies a death which dreams of When the vitality of your life shall be ever new.

4 Olive U

You are within all of my wishes,
you are thru-out all of my dreams,
you are the faithful purpose for kisses,
you are the truthful reason for extremes.

And when I close my eyes to wonder the hour of midnight,
I behold like a rainbow the sweet image of your heart's ambitions.
For these are as the universe's stars which shine so very bright;
a view that permits an honest understanding of your spirit's intentions.

You are within all of my prayers,
you are thru-out all of my dear-addresses,
you are the thoughtful one who cares,
you are the beautiful one who keeps promises.

And when I open my eyes to ponder the dawn of daylight,
I behold like a sun shower the picture of your mind's aspirations.
For these are as the sands of time so coupled with all insight;
a view that permits a sincere understanding of your soul's admiration.

mere observations | Ψ

Above and Beyond

α *Time and Space Beholding:*
Sincerely a pleasure for so many days...
that all conceptions of time and space belong no longer under it's essence.
For as I looked truthfully within every direction,
it was There and Then I did behold the sacred mystery...
that your Life New does sustain all that which is above and beyond compare.

Ω *Date and Place Unfolding:*
Honestly a treasure in so many ways...
that all perceptions of date and place no longer belong unto it's substance.
For all I peered faithfully thru-out every reflection,
it was Where and When I did unfold the blessed secrecy...
that your Love True does maintain all that which is above and beyond despair.

Above and Beyond II

Above perfection
and beyond deception
you define the purest image;
a design which is the truest picture.

Above flawlessness
And beyond lawlessness
you refine the surest knowledge;
an aged wine which is the sweetest tincture.

Unity of Being:
Purity of heart
is love's every part.
Clarity of mind
is truth's every find.
Security of soul
is faith's every control.
Sincerity of spirit
is life's every secret.
Decision is: Know Choice…
for the Realignment of the Vertical
is to bring Agreement to the Horizontal.

Acknowledgement

Enter: Sir Esse Ens
Circumnavigating the great event horizon of the universe;
comprehending it's relation to the timelessness of eternity.

As Time passed
And Space amassed
I accepted that this succession
was the grand scheme of all things.

For just as the absence of twilight is midnight
from all that is dusk unto all that is dawn;
as I traversed the great plain of this horizon
I realized that You are a necessity unto all that is my perpetuity.

As objects acquiesced
And subjects evanesced
I respected that this progression
was what it does seem of all things.

For just as the presence of insight is so right
from all that is life unto all that is death;
as I breathed the honest truths of every breath
I recognized that You are a sweet reality unto all that is my continuity.

Exit: Sir Esse Ens
Circumcontemplating the present liaison with the cosmos;
understanding it's re-creation to be the ultimate superlative.

Ψ | mere observations

Amidst Treachery

When surrounded by another's betrayal
it is so troublesome to forget all that which has become hatred;
yet thru-out the sands of history your kisses have remained sweetest.
When confounded by the other's denial
it is so meddlesome to remember all that was once sacred;
yet within the hands of mystery your promises have explained the deepest.

When astounded by another's deceit
it is so terrible to regret all that which has become treason;
yet thru-out the lands of no glory your stars have remained the brightest.
When dumbfounded by other's conceit
it is so horrible to surrender all that which was once reason;
yet within the brands of misery your scars have explained the highest.

Butterfly Kisses

α

Amidst the future of our history
a thousand days is a million years;
yet your butterfly kisses transcend time and space,
for within the twinkling of an eye I am purely conformed…

Unto all that is your Love True.

Ω

Amidst the nature of our mystery
a thousand ways is a million tears;
yet your butterfly kisses expand date and place,
for thru-out the inkling of a sigh I am surely transformed…

Unto all that is your Life New.

Diamond Tear Drops

Without understanding you
my words possess none,
yet explain their meaninglessness.
Without comprehending you
my deeds confess one,
yet retain their meaninglessness.

α

If I were to try to surely explain
a raybeam's spectrum of light glistening
upon the diamond teardrops of the mourning dew,
without the mystery of your admiration ever near,
all of my words would fall into sure obscurity
and cease to possess the relevance of their acute meaning.

Without your presence designed my dearest
I am like a lock disclosed yet devoid of it's key revealed.
For without the loveliness of your company given,
my inspiration could never hope to be opened completely.
So I request you to silently talk and converse of God with me
while the poetry of your quiet eloquence unbinds
the intricately defined essence of what is my very heart so sweetly.

Ω

If I were to try to purely retain
a daydream's sanctum of night listening
unto the diamond teardrops of the storming blue,
without the novelty of your aspirations ever here,
all of my deeds would rise into pure absurdity
and cease to witness the importance of their astute dreaming.

Without your absence assigned to my nearest
I am like a lock enclosed yet devoid of it's key concealed.
For without the loneliness of your truancy taken,
my captivation could never hope to be fastened discretely.
So I request you to patiently walk and disperse abroad with me
while the symmetry of your violet elegance unwinds
the delicately refined substance of what is my every part so neatly.

Enslaved to Freedom

I am bound by the laws
which govern the reality of my very heart and mind;
so ruled by the perfected flaws,
by all the questions lost that the answer's reply cannot seem to find.

I am freed by the graces
which liberate the identity of my very spirit and soul;
so filled are the empty spaces,
with all the solution's cost that the problem's outcry only used to control.

Equiponderance
A state in which two sides are equally balanced.

α *Metaphysical Contemplation of the Heavens Above:*
Enter: Sir Esse Ens
"As light travels so the great measure of the Milky Way,
how I do wish to drink of your beautiful mind and spirit."

A Thought Between a Thought:
Yes, you are the accurate numbers upon my sun's dial.
For although it is an X amount of light years unto the nearest star,
beyond Time and/or the shadow of a doubt I would journey all of Space,
the length and breadth of the universe, any great distance just to be with you.

Ω *Supernatural Meditation upon all Life and Love:*
Exit: Sir Esse Ens
"As night marvels at the great treasure of the silky day,
how I do dream and think of your wonderful heart in secret."

A Dream Between a Dream:
Know, you are the correct letters of law by which I am brought to trial.
For my defense is ever close to the judgement that you are the dearest by far,
above perceived guilt and innocence I would search for evidence in every place,
the height and depth of the cosmos, just to prove the fact that I truly do love you.

*Amidst the pleasure of this balance of probabilities,
yes I do measure and glance at all possibilities.*

Frankincense and Myrrh

Purely, your eyes stir my remembrance
with an everlasting whirlpool of sweet memory;
milk and honey so deep and free of every encumbrance
that I immerse myself and wash away all of this earthly misery.

As I bathe and contemplate the reality of my sorrow's acquiescence,
the enlightened streams of your insight utter intricate simplicities unto me.
For within the rushing transcendence of your waters of loving-compassion,
a flowing purity conceals the disclosed secrecy of your wondrous deeds...
indescribable.

Surely, your eyes are frankincense and myrrh;
incense lamps whose spectra fragrantly fill the mind and spirit.
You are true vision amidst myopic sight so obscure;
a niagara of symmetry unto all those who admire thee kind in secret.

While I lay and meditate the finality of my sorrow's evanescence,
the enbrightened springs of your insight utter delicate complexities unto me.
For thru-out the gushing resplendence of your rivers of living-devotion,
a growing surety reveals the enclosed mystery of your splendrous needs...
inexpressible.

From Alpha to Omega

α First-Perfection:
"I wish that you could understand…

Yes, I have loved you from the very beginning
and shall beyond the unfolding of our history's end.
It was never a matter of a lost heart winning
for within your spirit I found the embodiment of a true friend.

When you and I poured ourselves unto each other,
Time and Space coalesced and commenced to actually exist;
for the essence of nothing else became more real than another.
Like the lonely pain that a lover would discover and feel
when their dear counterpart is away and is factually missed:
an absolute refining of character the crucible of this sorrow would sweetly reveal.

Ω Last-Completion:
…your wish is my every command."

Know, I have lived you from the very start
and shall above the beholding of our mystery's very finish.
It was never a matter of mending a broken heart
for thru-out your command you complemented my soul's every wish.

When you and I became complete as one together,
Date and Place convalesced and proceeded to possess meaning;
for the substance of this moment meant that sum forever.
Like the good pleasure that a lover would recover and seal
there before here after he or she realized they were not dreaming:
an ultimate defining of existence the reality of this morrow would deeply conceal.

From Cause to Effect: A Priori
Using a cause to form a judgement about probable results: the effect.

Your **Love True** is the Cause
and my **Life New** is the due Effect;
These are the universal laws
that I have discerned,
which I have discovered,
that I have so learned,
which I have uncovered,
and thus…
have understood with the utmost respect.

Grand Expectation

α

Life may not be what I wish it to be.
Yet whatever the severity of the circumstance
there is one thing that is eternally for certain: You.
For within the soul's will of my spirit's volition
this is sincerely all that I have learned to accept as new.

Ω

Love may not be what I dream it to be.
Yet whatever the insanity of the encumbrance
there is one thing that shall always purely remain: You.
For thru-out the heart's choice of my mind's recognition
this is honestly all that I have discerned and respect as true.

Great Ambition

α

All of the things you have sought for,
these only give one the illusion of true peace.
For could you ever understand and accept it so sweetly
when another would forever demand and expect this to be
all of the things of impurity that it's essence can never truly plea?

Ω

All of the things you have fought for,
these only give one the delusion of new release.
For could you ever comprehend and respect it completely
when another would together befriend and accept this to be
all of the things of uncertainty that it's substance can never truly free?

In Order - Numpa Echaga

Through wear and tear
I must truly Be fair;
yes, I must let go of the past
in order to possess what the **True Future** holds.

Though worn and torn
I am purely twice Born;
yes, from the first unto the last
in order to access what the **New Nature** moulds.

In the Wake of Nature

Enter: Sir Esse Ens
Walking in a forest's warmth
amidst the silent cool of the evening.
Pondering notions of certainty
as the branches leaves whisper among themselves.

I perceived the chimes of the wind amidst the backdrop of the moonlit night;
the breeze animating the trees as silver lined clouds moved ever so slowly, rolling by.
Behind these, the stars in the heavens above shone alone their brilliant light;
while I breathed discernment in the crispness of the air's answer to every question why.

It was this moment at which You and I commenced to sincerely converse;
as miracles performed and prophecies conformed unto the fruition of their fulfillment.
For this was the instant that You and I solved great mysteries of the universe;
while ancient wisdom unfolded her hands presenting the gifts of every queries bestillment.

As spirits traversed and shadows walked into twilight,
excruciating pain fell from darkened shrouds of doom.
What was the ultimate meaning of this dire loneliness?
But dear moments to discover that You are indeed there, very aware.

While secrets conversed and silhouettes talked of all insight,
these tears, like rain, poured from blackened clouds of gloom.
What was the absolute purpose of those storms of sadness?
But clear instances to understand that You are in fact there, everywhere.

Exit: Sir Esse Ens
Sleeping peacefully under a tree as dawn breaks,
while dreaming of sailing the sea of tranquillity.

Je Ne Sais Quoi
I Know Not What

I am a bird within your sky
that I never cease to soar so very high.
I am a word thru-out your sigh
that I no longer choose to silently deny…
the truth of this sincerity.

I am a fish within your ocean
that I never cease to swim so very deep.
I am a wish thru-out your emotion
that I do stronger love the notions you keep…
the wisdom of that clarity.

You and I understood the inconsequence
which ebbs smoothly within each and every part defined.
The differentiation,
the contradistinction,
between love, hate and cool indifference,
which flows softly thru-out the union of one heart and mind.

L.O.Y.A.L.
Love Of Your Abundant Life

Just as the notions of my mind so admires
and so longs to truthfully understand the things of Your Spirit
purely within the depths of my very heart…
all that which is the love of Your abundant life is deeply concealed.

Just as the motions of my kind desires
and so yearns to faithfully comprehend the things of Your secret
surely thru-out the heights of my every part…
all that which is the life of Your abundant love is sweetly revealed.

Mere Thought and Feeling
Presently In Absentia.

Enter: Sir Esse Ens
"From the omnipresent mountain streams of faith,
Truth and freedom, there I sit and contemplate.
Unto the omniscient fountain springs of knowledge
and wisdom where I lay and meditate, hear me."

About you is all that I can wondrously think;
for you are like a river of certainty flowing thru-out my mind.
Of these crystalline waters is all I wish to drink;
for never another ebbing current purified do I ever dream to find.

Yes, you are like transcendence preciously thought;
for you define the highest conception
and absolute notion of all that is the sweetness of sure beauty.
Comprehend that your person is graciously sought;
for you refine the deepest perception
and ultimate emotion of all that is the completeness of pure duty.

About you is all that I can splendrously feel;
for Presently In Absentia you are an enigma within my very heart.
Yet all of the mystery that you secretly reveal
is concealed as a priceless treasure, a masterpiece, and a work of art.

Yes, you are like a heavenly promise and it's sealing;
for your existence reflects just like a mirror,
the essence and communication of all that is the sight of my vision.
Understand that your spirit is so worth unveiling;
for your consistence respects just so sincerer
the presence and manifestation of all that is the might of my mission.

Exit: Sir Esse Ens
"The brightest star in the heavens tonight
fails so in comparison to the true distance
that I surely would travel just to be by your side.
For I would transcend the speed of light
while circumnavigating the universe's existence
just to be the only one in whom you do truly confide."

mere observations | Ψ

Meta 4 U

Just as waters are for the seas,
I am a dolphin diving within the unfathomable depths of your ocean.
Just as winds are for the breeze,
I am an eagle soaring thru-out the unsearchable expanse of your sky.

Just as choices are for decisions,
this consequence remains all that is the deepest of every mystical notion.
Just as voices are for opinions,
this innocence explains all that is the sweetest of every supernatural high.

Music

Yes, you are music to the very soul of my spirit;
truly a transcend melody to the very heart of my mind.
A song that possesses my each and every thought;
like butterfly kisses enrapturing the depths of my existence.

Yes, you are music to the every goal of my secret;
truly a resplendent harmony to every part of my kind.
A song that caresses my each and every thought;
like butterfly kisses enrapturing the heights of my persistence.

mere observations | Ψ

14UNI2C
One for You and I to See

Yes, put me through the fire,
refine these perceptions that be unto the purest gold.
Thoughts of you I cannot retire,
for those conceptions that be influence all I do behold.

Such as the rising of the sun
to the setting of the semi-illuminated moon;
from the ebb and flow of the ocean
to all the stars that shine so very bright at noon.

Love True has surpassed each and every sanction,
for His loving kindness is truly above and beyond all human law.
Life New has encompassed each and every faction,
for His living finesse is purely above and beyond all human flaw.

7 Questions Answer
What is it that your person is searching for?
Can it be located within the parameters of the known universe?
Would one have to die to find it?
Would not one have to live to esteem it?
Is it situated outside the perimeters of the shown One-Disperse?
Would one have to sigh to remind it?
Would not one have to give to redeem it?

If it is The Understanding within **Love True** for which you are sojourning,
preciously, it can in fact only be your soul's privilege to possess this completely.
If it is The Undemanding thru-out **Life New** for which you are discerning,
graciously, it can in fact only be your goal's courage to caress that so sweetly.

Ψ | mere observations

Once Twice

I once had spoken with misery
professing that the objects of my dreams
had been impatiently crushed under the weight of pain.
She gave me a sincere reply proclaiming,
"Could anything in one's life ever be completely sacred
when one is madly in love with the indifference to their self-hatred?"

I once had written to mystery
confessing that the subjects of my themes
had been consequently flushed down the proverbial drain.
She sent me a honest reply exclaiming,
"Could anyone have made wisdom their intimate friend
without understanding that not only the lonely do truly comprehend?"

Sir Esse Ens of Esprit de Corps

...of the Spirit

Faithfully of the Spirit
nothing about Life New is impossible.
So please my love, remain here with me
within the Confidence of all that is purely conceivable.

Truthfully of the Spirit
everything about Love True is attainable.
So I ask you my life, remain there with me
thru-out the Reliance of all that is surely perceivable.

Graciously of the Spirit
nothing about Life New is improbable.
So please my love, stay very near to me
within the Acceptance of all that is sincerely believable.

Preciously of the Spirit
everything about Love True is obtainable.
So I ask you my life, stay very dear to me
thru-out the Assurance of all that is honestly achievable.

Nocturne

As my mind contemplated you
amidst the flawless hours of the moon last night,
the dichotomy of the dawning sun
distressed the ideal visions of you within my weary eyes.
While my heart meditated true
the captivation of these thoughts until first light,
the epiphany of those realizations won
wished to express themselves to you if it should also arise.

And if it should be that the instance
of this ever inclusive moment shall never come,
then the essence of these confessions
would sojourn thru-out the spectral horizon a little longer.
And if it should be that the distance
of this ever elusive extent doubles it's sum,
again the substance of those admissions
would discern that conviction can only grow a lot stronger.

As certainty surpasses the temporal nature
of all beautiful things brought into existence,
nothing shall destroy the renewed purity of dreaming
within a redeemed soul's core of imperishable emotion.
While thoughts do flow like a river's mixture
into deep oceans of a sweet notion's consistence,
only one shall employ the valued clarity of meaning
thru-out an esteemed mind's lore of invariable devotion.

Death may die
and life may live
yet I preciously understand
that I shall always faithfully love you.

Orchestration of the Constellations

Enter: Sir Esse Ens
Conducting metaphysically the symphony of the universe
as every object within the perimeter expresses it's composition.

α Time and Space Beholding:
The absence of your person purely extracted
along with the presence of mine perfectly sync'd,
permit me to quench this insatiable thirst
and drink of your stream of subconsciousness.
For Here and Now amidst the resplendent factuality of There and Then,
Time and Space do become the milk and honey mixture of their gracious essence.

As light honestly brightens the spectrum of our event horizon,
to yet understand wondrously the very heart of your sweet perceptions,
while beholding these possibilities within the very mind of my conceptions,
so it is and for always will be the viceless expression of all that is an eternal pleasure.

Ω Date and Place Unfolding:
The existence of your being surely enacted
along with the consistence of mine flawlessly linked,
permit me to wake that palatable first
and think of your dream of true-consciousness.
For clearly how amidst the transcendent actuality of Where and When,
Date and Place do become the gold and diamond fixture of their precious substance.

As truth sincerely enlightens the wisdom of our present union,
to yet comprehend splendrously the very soul of your smooth reflections,
while unfolding those probabilities thru-out the very spirit of my impressions,
so it is and for all days will be the priceless possession of all that is an eternal treasure.

Exit: Sir Esse Ens
Directing supernaturally the symmetry of the One-Disperse
as every subject thru-out that parameter confesses it's disposition.

Praecaedere

The precise moment that I ceased to be inspired
by worthlessness of self and my ill perceived lack thereof.
Before the twinkling of an eye, I preciously aspired
to purely desire and seek after all those things which you love.

Wherewithal that is my soul as this mysterious plot thickened,
your sincerity of heart is all that I wished to sweetly drink.
Therewithal that is my spirit as this wondrous thought so quickened,
your security of mind is all that I dreamed to deeply think.

Yet, for the definite lack of a better descriptive word
I cannot illustrate or properly interpret all that you mean to me.
Logically I am not permitted to dwell upon the absurd
but to fulfill all that you need is more than a selfish want for me.

Someone has said that honesty brings insight unto the blind;
if that is so, then understand the vision that I miraculously see.
For the eyes of truth have filled my being with notions so kind;
with beautiful images of all the things that you and I could possibly be.

Psi Quotiens

To dream is to drink of the surety of your potions;
for the sweet elixir of your disposition is so breath taking.
The theme is to think of the purity of your notions;
for the honey mixture of your temperaments are so life giving.

The wish is to desire all of your milky soft lotions;
for the warmed remedy of your true devotion is so heart breaking.
The hope is to acquire all of your silky smooth motions;
for the formed harmony of your measurements are so mind fixing.

Ψ | mere observations

Relative Relation

α
What is the conception of Time and Space
relative to the Absoluteness of Your Mind's omniscience?
But that which ebbs and flows consistently new.
For what is the true-essence of love's spirituality
in relation to the gracious wisdom of Your truth's revelation?
But that which has been eternally defined and forever esteemed.

Ω
What is the perception of Date and Place
relative to the Ultimateness of Your Heart's omnipresence?
But that which keeps and knows persistently true.
For what is the new-substance of life's universality
in relation to the precious system of Your star's constellation?
But that which has been eternally refined and together redeemed.

Reunion

Reunited after many years,
the separation became so unbearable.
A sacrifice of plenty tears,
the reparation became incomparable.

All I could do was think of you.
All I could do was feel for you.
All I could do was pray for you.
All I could do was seal my love for you.

All I could do…
Yes, all I would do.

Spectrum

α *Expanding the Prism:*
Yes, within your divine sublimity
I purely wondered over it's concealed meaning;
encased by the brightest of all light
my very heart did unfold the heights of your freedom.

Ω *Transcending the Prison:*
Know, thru-out your sublime divinity
I surely pondered under it's revealed dreaming;
erased by the darkest of all night
my every part did behold the depths of your wisdom.

mere observations | Ψ

Stepping Stones Skipping Upon
the Rippling Waters of Time and Space

α

From the fountain of the deepest sigh
when making every wrong thing right;
unto a heart that Here is understanding
within a soul that Now is undemanding.

Amidst the magical succession of coming events,
the glory of the stars are yours and mine tonight;
as the sweet consummations of twilight illuminates
the union of our personalities enjoined when soon we do become one.

Ω

From the mountain of the sweetest high
when making every dark thing light;
unto a mind that There is comprehending
thru-out a spirit that Then is so unending.

Amidst the logical progression of passing moments,
the story of the scars and wounds shine so bright;
as the dear illumination of insight reanimates
the horizon of our identities under the moon which is ruled by the sun.

That Which Is, Thereof

When so it seems truly agreed
that the woven fabric of all time and space
has itself arbitrarily disagreed
and thus consequently comes to a grinding halt.

Regardless of superficial concerns
which in fact have lost their usual place
or the circumstance that never learns
when one's conscience is so logically finding fault.

Yes, it is indeed by the precious arrangement
of the sweet composition of your mind and spirit
that I am no longer inspired by estrangement
but by your beautiful unity of being and all that you do sincerely wonder.

Considerate of diverse thoughts and feelings
that your complex heart and soul wish to keep secret.
curiously I am intrigued by these concealings
and by your rivers teeming with mystery and all that you do honestly ponder.

The Companion of Loneliness

State of the art,
fate of the kind.
State of the heart,
fate of the mind.

So many memories of you that remind
yet I must leave the sorrows of the past far behind.
For love now shines brightly and evenly within daylight
whether or not my very heart has accepted it's poverty or wealth.

So many miseries at par that are unkind
yet I just leave the shadows which are cast undefined.
For love here shines rightly and heavenly thru-out midnight
whether or not my every part has affected it's sickness or health.

So many memories of you that remind
yet I must leave the morrows of the last far behind.
For love now shines brightly and evenly within sun showers
whether or not my very spirit has respected the better or worse.

So many miseries at par that are unkind
yet I just leave the meadows which are passed unrefined.
For love here shines rightly and heavenly thru-out moon hours
whether or not my every secret has effected the blessing or curse.

For love.

Ψ | mere observations

The Dolphin and the Eagle Aforementioned
An Epilogue to Meta 4 U

Just to think conceptions of you so true
and the acknowledged mind aforementioned does ever wonder;
for like a dolphin descending a great ocean
there the dearest memory of your perfection is the deepest notion.

Just to feel perceptions of you so true
and the encouraged heart aforementioned does ever ponder;
for like an eagle ascending a grand quotient
there the sweetest mystery of your devotion is the highest emotion.

mere observations | Ψ

The Everlasting To Be

The way I used to think,
I do not think those ways anymore.
Time was in and out of sync
when my true devotion came after all that was surely not before.

Yet there was a time
when I thought that you might return;
and so was the crime
that I failed to see the insight of the climb where I would discern:

Above all that is word and deed,
beyond all that is want and need,
we are to understand the essence of this milk and honey mixture:
To Be is to live and make **Love True** within all that is **The Everlasting**.

The day I used to feel,
I do not feel those days anymore.
Space could no longer conceal
when my new emotion went after all that was purely sought before.

Yet there was a space
when I felt that you might return;
and so was the grace
that I prevailed to see the twilight of the place where I would sojourn.

Above all that is said and done,
beyond all that is some and none,
we are to comprehend the substance of this gold and diamond fixture:
To Be is to eternally give and take **Life New** thru-out all that is **The Everlasting**.

The Oracle of Sir Esse Ens

Enter: Sir Esse Ens
"The universe as such
is merely but a well oiled machine;
designed to move as much
upon the sum total and equilibrium of all it's parts.

Knowledge diverse is discerned
within created minds from all that is seen;
wisdom being kinetically learned
and defined thru-out the medium of sincere hearts."

I am the sun,
I am the moon,
I am the stars,
shining bright at noon.

I am truly the creation,
an Ex Nihilo manifestation.
From me your body was born,
because of rebellion, I am torn.

When He gave you your breath,
it was then that there was no death.
But now I too am fallen in shame,
and so reserved for the intense flame.

Yet you are redeemed within such elegance,
for you are esteemed thru-out much relevance.
Although some fates may not be the same,
His grace has released you from all of the blame.

Exit: Sir Esse Ens
"I wait for Him to come,
He Who is called Faithful.
I do yearn for freedom
in Him Who is called Truthful."

The Risen Son vs The Fallen One
*Thoughts above and beyond normal comprehension,
truly within and thru-out formal contemplation.*

We exist in a state of entropy
where things do inevitably tend to fall apart.
Yes, a Time and Space entwined,
with a Date and Place combined;
where my enemy pretends to Be
a true Until-The-End friend of me
but then in front of my back, breaks my very heart.

The Truth - Word and Deed

Understand the truth within my eyes;
conceal thru-out your very spirit all that you do perceive.
All that my vision-seeing longs to tell you
shall be said silently with words that desire you to acknowledge… forever.

While I breathe the sure essence of your sighs,
reveal unto my very heart all that you do wish to achieve.
All that my mission-being yearns to show you
will be done quietly with deeds that request you to encourage… eternally.

Comprehend the truth within my eyes;
enclose thru-out your every secret all that you do conceive.
All that my person-giving longs to tell you
shall be said loudly with words that desire you to always accept… forever.

While I breathe the pure substance of your sighs,
disclose unto my every part all that you hope to receive.
All that my notion-living yearns to show you
will be done proudly with deeds that request you to always respect… eternally.

Within the spirituality of this factuality so true,
you and I truthfully possess the confession of this mystery:
one heart,
one mind,
and one body wondrously conformed unto that of the other.

Thru-out the universality of this actuality so new,
you and I faithfully witness the profession of this secrecy:
one soul,
one spirit,
and one breath splendrously transformed unto that of the other.

The Union of Wisdom and Knowledge

α The Bride, Wisdom, speaks:
Permit us to embrace the vast emptiness of Space
so coupled with the passage of every moment of Time.
For within the logical conception of our notions combined,
let us behold the mystery of all that is synchronous and symmetrical.

You and I have become one enlightened rationality,
an ultimate recognition of all that is factually known to be Real.
For while the circumference of the universe expands,
together we unfold the measurements of our Reality's perfected dimensions:

Eternal Life New.

Ω The Groom, Knowledge, replies:
Permit us to welcome the illumination of every place,
as heaven's light emitted fills the spectrum of creation sublime.
For thru-out the magical perception of our motions entwined,
let us behold the secrecy of all that is synonymous and not accidental.

You and I have become one enlightened personality,
an absolute recognition of all that is actually shown to be Ideal.
For while the complements of the cosmos understands,
forever we unfold the wonderment of our Identity's accepted perfections:

Eternal Love True.

The Valley of the Shadow of Death

Here, this place where I have fallen
into the deep valley far below the snow-capped mountains;
hear, I do, the voice of the spirit within
querying my soul to drink of the waters of life's fountains.

Consequences bring one's tears to many places
where experience forces plenty where they do not wish to go;
yet how we are all reminded of our Lord's graces,
for the Spirit uses things we truly do not wish to know.

I am not alone,
for I have you right by my side.
I am not on my own,
for I can see that you are my guide.

Such a cool breeze
as tears trickle down a lost child's cold face.
Bent on my knees
like the same child asking for one warm embrace.

Why is it that I have fallen so far away
wandering off to some great desolate land?
Why have I walked from the light of the day
wondering if the night's sorrow will let go of my hand?

Yet, how sweet and patient you are.

Thoughts Become

Without knowing you
my life is devoid of meaning.
Without showing you
my love is devoid of dreaming.

α *Conceptions Unfolding*
Alone within my war torn reflections unrefuted,
sweet conceptions of your perfections designed are all I can truthfully achieve.
For just the thought of your image's elegance undiluted
becomes the potent cause and effect of all that defines the essence of my existence.

Yet mere words could never amount the factuality of those expressions,
of how I wish to know the aspirations of your mind's notions so beautifully enclosed.
For I hope that I may be able to understand with utmost certainty
the ultimate disposition of the sweetest convictions of your very heart metaphysically revealed.

Ω *Perceptions Beholding:*
Alone thru-out my forlorn impressions undisputed,
dear perceptions of your dimensions assigned are all that I can faithfully receive.
For just the thought of your knowing's brilliance attributed
becomes the cogent laws and respect of all that refines the substance of my consistence.

Yet clear deeds could only account the actuality of those confessions,
of why I wish to show the admiration of your kind's motions so wonderfully disclosed.
For I hope that I may be able to comprehend with utmost clarity
the absolute intimation of the purest intentions of your every part supernaturally concealed.

Thoughts Become - The Reprise

Yes, the very question of you
beckons within me an answer never required;
for the very mention of you
reckons thru-out me it's query ever admired.

α *Purest Eyes of the Deepest Blue:*
Amidst the flawless arrangement
of all that has become an immaculate perfection,
the undying devotion of the vision of your insightful youth
explains within my very heart and mind all that is the highest factuality.

If my purest intention should ever eloquently come unprofessed,
more than evidently, do permit your aspirations to meditate upon this flowing continuity.
For just to barely understand the symmetry of your beautiful image,
my thoughts do become like the ones whose gracious words and deeds are no longer uninspired.

Ω *Surest Sighs of the Sweetest True:*
Amidst the lawless estrangement
of all that has become an elaborate deception,
the unlying position of the mission of your delightful truth
sustains thru-out my every part so kind all that is the deepest actuality.

If my surest ambition would ever consequently go unconfessed,
more than apparently, do permit your admirations to contemplate upon this growing perpetuity.
For just to rarely comprehend the poetry of your wonderful knowledge,
my thoughts do become like the ones whose precious wants and needs are no longer undesired.

To Sense - Pennies from Heaven

Sadly while I observe you slipping thru my hands,
the very breath of my spirit gasps and barely understands.
Even though I realize that we are just good friends,
the very breadth of my secret grasps and rarely comprehends.

Yes, with all that is the soul of your very heart,
my how I do desire a genuine conversation so much sweeter.
For it seems that our persons only discuss the surface
when we should be graciously tasting the honey of **Life New**.

Indeed I have wished that your person perceived and knew.
Know I have prayed that your being would meditate upon this act:
intact the contents of the essence of my existence is to love you,
for I have dreamt that your being would truly recognize this fact.

Yes, with all that is the whole of your every part,
my how I do require a mastermind contemplation so much deeper.
For it deems that our persons only mistrust the justice
when we should be preciously exploring the depths of **Love True**.

Ψ | mere observations

To You for You

Enter: Sir Esse Ens
"To die for you
is to live for you.
To sigh for you
is to breathe for you."

When encouraging the want and the need
of all that has become my dire lack of motivation,
permit my very heart and mind to call upon their inspiration
that I may be able to show and tell you within this word and deed.
For as those combined do strengthen all that is my mission's being,
the enlightening might of your flawless symmetric wonder
thru-out my every part so kind becomes all that is so eternally precious.

When acknowledging the some and the none
of all that has become my dire lack of captivation,
permit my very soul and spirit to fall upon their admiration
that I may be able to know as well you within this said and done.
For as these entwined do lengthen all that is my vision's seeing,
the enbrightening sight of your faultless poetic splendor
thru-out my every goal so secret becomes all that is so eternally gracious.

Exit: Sir Esse Ens
"To you my **Life New**,
for you I shall always live.
Yes, with you I will always give.
To you my **Love True**,
for you I shall always care.
Yes, with you I will always share."

Unprecedented

Yes, I remember that you were the only one
who stood out from the rest of the crowd's "everyone else".
Possessing a grace not aware of just your person
truly nothing compared to the precious sharing of yourself.

While my heart held on to the possibility
of definitely letting the memory of you go completely,
I realized that you gave me a sense of family
for the combined life of your love graciously set me free.

Continually for you there remains a tear in my eye,
an echoing loneliness that fills my each and every step.
Perpetually for you there explains a thorn in my sigh
that amidst empty moments I foolishly wish we never met.

Yet these thoughts of you are like milk and honey,
like when a new born babe tastes of them at first chance.
Sweet as the dew of summer days warm and sunny,
like when a true born being feels the light of a second glance.

Ψ | mere observations

Welcome

I. Inception:
Believe you me truly,
for I wish to conceal myself
within all that is your secret.
For the reticent words that you fluently speak
are the dialects of eloquence that my silence wants to learn.

II. Reception:
Receive you me purely,
for I dream to reveal myself
thru-out all that is your spirit.
For the quiescent deeds that you prudently seek
are the heavenly body languages that my person needs to discern.

III. Conception:
Conceive you me dearly,
for I desire to present myself
unto all that is your mind.
For the thoughts of love which you preciously think
are the notions that still the uncertainties stirring within my intelligence.

IV. Perception:
Perceive you me surely,
for I aspire to entrust myself
unto all that is your kind.
For the streams of life which you graciously drink
are the fountains that fill the estuaries flowing thru-out my true-existence.

When Again

When again all I can do is sit and patiently wait;
like thistles, how these feelings of anxiety do ever plague one so.
Yet your love shall always remain my central concern,
for this could never be only a peripheral return…of mere emotion.
Please my dearest, all you must do is trust,
for I would indeed give you my left hand
and show you with the right that I do understand your spirit's every devotion.

When again all I can do is quietly contemplate;
like thorns, how these thoughts of perplexity do ever like to grow.
Yet your love shall always explain my primary regard,
for this could never be only a secondary award…for mere endurance.
Please my nearest, all you just do is trust,
for I would in fact take you to be my woman
and promise you that I am always to be your man, no matter what the encumbrance.

Ψ | mere observations

COLLECTION TWO
Sir Dreadlee Groove Esq.

2 Olive U II

A Wish - Beginning to End

A Rose and Twelve Kisses

All Things Considered

An Orderly Perplexity*

Changeless Truth for Changing Times

Circumspect

Even Essence: The Gist of a Tear Drops Mist

Faith

F.E.A.R.?

From the Deepest Commitment Unto the Sweetest Contentment

Illumination

Indifference vs Inconsequence

Law of Liberty

Megahertz

Mourning - Wife

Mourning - Mother

Mourning - Friend

Paradoxology

Presently an Absentee

Precisely the Truth

Repentance vs Remorse

Remorse de Prefoundis

Sanctuary

The Antithesis of Certainty

The Difference

The 'I' of the Storm

The Present Gift of a Future Past The Day After the Night Before Last*

The World

This Sorrow

Thrice the Gist*

Truth for You

Interactive Poem

mere observations | Ψ

2 Olive U II

Yes, I do wonder where you are;
when will all of you return to me?
For I do ponder precisely how far
to how much closer you could possibly be.

So near...
like two as one.
So dear...
like we had already done.

Yes, I do admire who you are;
when will all of you come back to me?
For I do desire to know how far
to how much closer you shall become free.

So distant...
like two who have parted ways.
So persistent...
like you and I were for so many days.

Yet here and now both they and you are gone
like night that cruelly will not return unto dawn.

A Wish - Beginning to End

I wish that you could understand.
I wish that you would comprehend.
I wish that you could take my hand.
I wish that you would see I am your friend.

Words can look so good written down,
even better when they are spoken correctly.
Yet let me emphasize this with a serious frown
and declare that my actions will be true directly.

But this remains to be purely seen,
for it demands to be proven within known actuality.
I must say and do what I truly mean,
for this is required to be shown thru-out all factuality.

A Rose and Twelve Kisses

The composition of my thoughts are arranged
by the vision of your beautiful style and grace.

And when I close my eyes to dream
I discover revealed…the image of you.
Four times three I conceal a glance at your enchanting smile
that silently speaks so eloquently unto all.
You truly possess an elegant spirit
that is filled with the secret of loving kindness.
For all that is your every part's living finesse overflows freely
from your very heart's out pouring cup.

And when I observe mystically
the twinkling stars during a clear night's sky,
the wind brings forth your fragrance in streams so real
that I open my mouth in admiration to taste it.
Yes, it is indeed the Life New of your goal
and the Love True of your soul.
Nothing compares to all that explains the breath-taking essence
of the inspiration of your being.

And when I am enraptured by the warmth
of these mysterious ocean side breezes,
only thoughts of you dance like trickling rain with my emotions
in all of The Everlasting's notions.
Therefore, my enraptured heart's commitment
lays a precious flower upon your thigh,
while the embrace of my spirit's contentment
presents your gift with the pledge of twelve endless kisses.

And when I kiss the presence of your absence
whispering softly thru-out my care,
each of those vows sigh desiring only the satisfying fruit
of your faithful word's comforting solace.

mere observations

As I am felled by the harsh reality of knowing
that with someone else you share,
understand that I am a man that respects the truth
of all that your deeds have chosen to promise.

And when I take view of the Father's orchestration
of the ordained constellations,
I am truly blessed that my perceptions can recall such elaborate details
of your incomparable beauty.
For it is then that I am truly unblinded and see
your person's Ne Plus Ultra sincerity.
Yes…nothing, not even my despair, shall ever compare
to all the things you are, not only unto me.

I, my dearest, do lay the most truthful flower
to rest upon your uncertainties sigh.
I do present your loving tenderness with every consummating kiss
that Life New and Love True possesses.
Permit me to give you the rest of my days
within and thru-out the best of their ways.
For I hope and wish that you and I will be able to purely understand
the master plan and all that it caresses.

And when I give praise to the only enlightened star
within the heavens above,
my declaration thru-out the existence of the expanding universe
shall remain one and the same.
Once upon a contemplation, you and I became a decision
of unprecedented certainty.
Living and loving together united as one body forevermore
within and thru-out The Everlasting's name.

2u4u Skye Rose

Sir Dreadlee Groove Esq.

All Things Considered

I do like all of the things that you like,
for I do love all of the things that you love.
Sometimes we may agree to disagree alike,
yet I see your dreams to be what inspiration is made of.

Understand that I do possess aspirations of my own
and that I never live vicariously thru your personality.
But I am in conformance with all things known
about all the wishes that your being hopes to make a reality.

Not that my mind exists within a sphere of fantasy
or that my very heart accepts the limitations of impossibility.
Not that my kind persists thru-out a realm of fallacy
or that my every part respects the imitations of improbability.

For the beauty of your love is so sweet
that you make this very definition weak.
It requests to re-define itself and speak
about how it's reinterpretation is left in speechlessness.

Yes, the duty to your life is so complete
that you make this very devotion strong.
It requests to re-strengthen itself and belong
unto all the things of patience, sacrifice, and true selflessness.

An Orderly Perplexity

α
And when to my heart I do remain
every other place where you are not,
all that should be truthfully said my dearest
becomes an eloquence that words spoken could never express.
For when I am again astounded by your presence,
thoughts of you come further and enrapture me within speechlessness.

Ω
And when to my soul I do explain
every other space where you are sought,
all that should be faithfully done my nearest
becomes a consequence that vows broken could only witness.
For when I am again surrounded by your absence,
thoughts of you go farther and enrapture me thru-out deedlessness.

mere observations | Ψ

Changeless Truth for Changing Times

Please, be true to your first and last word.
Say all that you mean and mean all that you say.
These foolish lies shall only remain absurd.
For you understand that the truth is the only way.

undistorted
uncontorted

The tears flowing endlessly from my eyes
speak volumes on the love which I do possess for you.
Yet while my broken spirit constantly sighs,
my heart is comforted in and supported by what is true.

undisturbed
unperturbed

The fact that you chose to maintain an indifferent subtlety
did not change the direction or rearrange the decision of my only choice.
Yet like a caged bird with clipped wings who longed to soar free,
I became a deaf mute desiring to hear the sound of his own voice.

undaunted
unhaunted

Could your being take the time to listen to what silent consequences deem?
Would your person give a few moments to understand
the echoing sound of loneliness?
For those together proclaim that life is no longer just what it used to seem;
that your existence, amidst the vanity of the insanity,
has forgotten the essence of love's holiness.

questionably
unanswered, again.

Circumspect

In my deep loss
I truly have gained,
for I behold the cross
upon which all life and love is attained.

Though sure death
will inevitably strike,
to love You in health
I shall in the strife of my illness alike.

For what is the meaning of pleasure?
Yes, just what is the purpose of pain?
But that which has come forth
to query the heart of one's treasure.
Yet what shall define it's worth
but all that the fire refines to eternally remain.

Even Essence:
The Gist of a Tear Drops Mist

I will learn to abide Space and Time
before ascending the anger of these rigorous mounts of impatience.
I shall discern and not cease to truly climb
after descending the danger of those vigorous peaks of consequence.

I understand that your decision is in fact final,
for I sincerely do concur and will belong only unto my misery's acquiescence.
I comprehend that your choices are indeed vital,
for I honestly do agree and shall belong only unto your memory's evanescence.

Although it is so cold and so lonely without you,
certainly I contemplate true the warmth of the factuality that I am not so alone.
For I do see what is real and shall never doubt you,
again when I meditate new the strength of the actuality that I am not on my own.

The heart is breaking
while the mind is storming,
although loneliness is not absent,
yet within prayer, I am always here for you.

The soul is aching
while the spirit is forming,
although happiness is not present,
yet thru-out prayer, I am always here for you.

Ψ | mere observations

Faith

Within my deep sorrow and grief,
yes, you had a firm hold of my hand.
When tomorrow there was no relief,
you became my legs in order to help me stand.

And so it had begun:

As I beheld the setting of the sun,
you saw how I mourned this great loss.
While I hoped truly in the Risen One,
again you helped me to see the victory of the cross.

And I thank You:

For mine eyes turned unto the things eternal;
upon the mysterious realities which are not plainly seen.
I understood then that the present misery is at best only temporal,
to dwell upon the invisible riches where unbroken hearts have not been.

F.E.A.R.?
False Evidence Appearing Real?

Reduced to mere lifeless items
of a once living but now loveless household.
Induced by F.E.A.R. and surface problems,
why did we refuse to see the divine solution unfold?

Behold:

Within sickness and health
take all the forks and spoons,
give away all the dear momentos.
Thru-out poverty and wealth
take all of Jupiter's moons,
give away the whole entire cosmos.

Why did we let our selfish pretensions
fight to be the very centre of the universe?
Such foolish preconceived misperceptions
which for better or worse...
yearned for power...
and turned the hour of the blessing into a curse.

From the Deepest Commitment
Unto the Sweetest Contentment

I am at a loss for sincere words
when I find that your absence is indeed so near.
Like an admiring flight of little birds
my heart understands your presence to be so dear.

Beloved, to whom everything I have so entrusted,
within all that is the secrecy of this acknowledgement.
I request your person to comprehend the truth of this divine fact:
for I do promise to always care for you, not only in sickness and health.

Permit me to love you for who you are
and not only for what you might one day be.
A healing wound leaves a painful scar,
if only to remind some of how it is they have become free.

Beloved, to whom everything I have so adjusted,
thru-out all that is the mystery of this encouragement.
I request your being to so befriend the faith of this genuine act:
for I do promise to always share with you, not only in poverty and wealth.

Illumination

You and I shall marvel within this intuitive fashion
and contemplate true the creature of our spiritual mysteries.
For all that we surely do not know about one another
will truthfully be all that we do wish to understand.
To sincerely ever partake of each other
like a giving sister of a sharing brother;
to splendrously behold the dear strength of a compassionate hand.

You and I shall travel thru-out this indicative action
and meditate new the feature of our universal secrecies.
For all that we purely do not show unto one another
will faithfully be all that we do hope to comprehend.
To honestly never forsake so each other
like a living father of a caring mother;
to wondrously unfold the sweet warmth of an affectionate friend.

Indifference vs Inconsequence

She had no true opinion;
neither was everything good,
nor was there anything bad.
No authority or dominion;
nothing ever made her happy,
nothing ever made her sad.

She existed within a sphere of indifference;
neither was something black,
nor was there anything white.
She persisted thru-out a realm of inconsequence;
nothing for her was ever wrong,
nothing for her was ever right.

mere observations | Ψ

Law of Liberty

Mea culpa,
sans peur et sans reproche.
I am guilty,
yet fearless and innocently beyond reproach.

I sincerely do plead guilty for my honesty
but I love you so innocently in the first degree.
The truth of these facts shall always remain;
brought before the court
whether or not this choice to love you is wrong or right.
For the truth of these acts shall always explain;
a faithful witness of the sort
regardless if the consequence for my soul shall be black or white.

A love's defense built upon the revealed evidence
of the heart and mind's concealed guilt and innocence.
A factuality that shall always remain;
sought before judge and jury
whether or not this decision to love you is good or bad.
An actuality that shall always explain;
the jealous of another's fury
regardless if the conscience of my spirit shall be happy or sad.

Megahertz

Infra red,
ultra blue,
supra dread,
to transcend all of this,
to comprehend all that is true.

Millions of mega hurts;
the days of my sorrow were turned to this wave length.
Alone as loneliness flirts;
the ways of tomorrow became my night's brave strength.

The courage to see thru all the pain
of a broken heart's epic so healed yet scarred
became the wisdom to inwardly succeed truthfully.
For this truth ultimately became a valuable pearl to guard
when the madness surrounding my person proved itself too hard.

The knowledge to be never the same
while so many excuses appeared to be good enough
became the freedom to outwardly proceed faithfully.
For that faith absolutely became a priceless diamond in the rough
when the sadness dumbfounding my being proved itself too tough.

But now, it is on to much better things
not fit for corrupt queens and kings.
It is on to a life worth living and caring for.
Yes, on to a love worth giving and sharing for.

Amen.

Mourning - Wife

I mourn the loss of my dear wife, my closest companion,
but again I will not be long within my sorrow and grief,
for I have understood that you belong unto redemption
that your spirit is preserved because of your life's only belief.

Although you have passed
through and beyond the valley of the shadow of death,
one day we will be together at last,
loving within and living thru-out the gift of eternal breath.

No person is below redemption
and no spirit is truly above it.
It is for us to know salvation
for all to understand and love it.

Mourning - Mother

I mourn the loss of my dear mother and closest companion,
but again I will not be long within my sorrow and grief,
for I have understood that you belong unto redemption
that your spirit is preserved because of your life's only belief.

Although you have passed
through and beyond the valley of the shadow of death,
one day we will be together at last,
loving within and living thru-out the gift of eternal breath.

No person is below redemption
and no spirit is truly above it.
It is for us to know salvation
for all to understand and love it.

Mourning - Friend

I mourn the loss of a dear friend and close companion,
but again I will not be long within my sorrow and grief,
for I have understood that you belong unto redemption
that your spirit is preserved because of your life's only belief.

Although you have passed
through and beyond the valley of the shadow of death,
one day we will be together at last,
loving within and living thru-out the gift of eternal breath.

No person is below redemption
and no spirit is truly above it.
It is for us to know salvation
for all to understand and love it.

Paradoxology

I am wishing-hoping upon You the highest star;
for You have indeed transcended the deepest of all wisdom.
There is no more pain, only joy in the dearest scar;
one that shall remind me always of the sweetest of all freedom.

I am no longer in need or want of a pure sign;
for I am now in possession of the truest of all insight:
yes…this being an article of faith.
I am no stronger than when in You secure and divine;
for the blinding darkness flees the brightest of all light:
know…this being an article of truth.

Surely where there are mountains,
there is the precious and much coveted gold.
Truly where there are fountains,
there is flowing mightily spring waters cold.

Just as the semi-illuminated moon
travels the great circumference and design of the earth,
every saint prays that You will return soon,
for Your presence is so much more than these defined are worth.

mere observations | Ψ

Presently an Absentee

The past…it is the past,
for all I do possess is the present.
At last…it is at last,
I shall love you always even if you are absent.

I loved you when we first met
and I have loved you ever since that time.
Yet how much longer I must regret
and pay with my life for yesterday's crime?

It shall be no longer.

The future…it is the future,
for all I do possess is the here and now.
This nature…it is so mature,
yet will I be able to make this clear somehow?

I cared for you when we first met
and I have always cared for you ever since that moment.
I only remember that we must forget
and forgive with open hearts yesterday's torment.

We shall be so stronger.

Ψ | mere observations

Precisely the Truth

Mere words could never convey
all that I do desire to truthfully tell you.
So permit me to be metaphysically enraptured by your attention,
by your sweet irreducible factor upon which all my other facts depend.

Yet…I do not wish to say too much
because of the factuality that most conversations possess no meaning.
However, your heart do I hope to touch
that we may understand and feel that reality is not just a fantasy dreaming.

Clear deeds could only portray
all that I do aspire to faithfully show you.
So permit me to be supernaturally enraptured by your perfection,
by your dear common denominator upon which all my other acts contend.

Yet…I do not request to know a lot
because of the actuality that some decisions confess no purpose.
However, your mind so I have sought
that we may comprehend and see that choice is not just a clown's three ring circus.

mere observations | Ψ

Repentance vs Remorse

What does it mean to be a person?
Does it mean that I am only remembered by the things I have done in the past?
I am a person in the sight of God because He has forgiven me of all my sins.
It is only the consequences of my actions that I must deal with.
The only thing that I fail to understand is how I am to deal with
these circumstances here and now.

What shall I do?

I have this picture of my ex-wife,
and it bothers me to no end that I have not had the opportunity to express
how sorry I am for the way things turned out between us.
I despise the fact that I have not had the actual chance to express how I feel.
I still hold these deep feelings for her, but I understand that all of that is past
and can never be real.
I know the door is closed and can never be reopened.
It saddens me that I cannot tell her how I feel.

Dear God what am I to do?

It seems I am always left with questions more than with answers.
The life I live now is mostly filled with regret about what happened in the past.
How do I escape the sorrow I have caused myself?

"And if it should be that I shall never see you again,
indeed I shall graciously apologize to you in heaven."

Remorse de Profoundis

And if I have ever senselessly neglected you,
then truthfully permit me to apologize so dearly…
for the existence of my life is nothing without yours,
so please forgive me for failing to purely provide my care.

And if I have ever relentlessly disrespected you,
again faithfully permit me to recognize sincerely…
that I was wrong.
I have been so wrong.
For the essence of my love is worthless without yours,
so please forgive me for failing to surely furnish my share.

And if I have ever unwittingly rejected you,
from blue seas, permit me to say that I am indeed sorry…
for the persistence of my heart is nothing without yours,
so please forgive me for failing to cherish all that is precious unto me.

And if I have ever unfittingly not protected you,
on bruised knees, permit me to make amends in a hurry…
because that is what is right.
And how seldom I have been right.
For the presence of my mind is valueless without yours,
so please forgive me for failing to nourish all that is gracious unto me.

Sanctuary

Yes, your love is my sanctuary;
a place where there is no need to hide.
For your life, I do thank you verily;
an empty space there you fill so deep inside.

When worldly life has indeed gone asunder,
your loving kindness is my very heart's only consolation.
For when earthly strife has taken it's plunder,
your loving tenderness is my every part's only alleviation.

What would I do without you?
Except to lay down my body and die.
Because of you…
I so surrender everything that is askew
and truthfully regret nothing that is undue.

Know, your love is my sanctuary as such;
a beautiful face that offers no want of a disguise.
For your life, I do thank you so very much,
your wonderful grace is given as a gift and not a prize.

When daily existence has fallen to pieces
and the night's puzzling shadow has cast it's dark affliction,
your persistence streams forth and releases,
like water, the light to shine upon all of the stark tribulation.

I could never ever doubt you,
except to give up my spirit and sigh.
Because of thee…
I so remember all good things sweetly,
yet faithfully forget all evil things completely.

The Antithesis of Certainty

I loved you with a love undying
but then this perception truly died,
and thus, a bright shadow was cast.
For I became so intoxicated with a sober mind
when I found lost all I could no longer afford to lose or find.

The sanity
amidst the reality
there was…
nevermore a place for you,
yet evermore a space for you.

I lived you with a life undenying
but then that conception was also denied,
and thus, a sigh breathed it's very last.
For I became so fixated with a broken heart
when I counted worthless the formerly appraised work of art.

The vanity
amidst the finality
there was…
nevermore a face for you,
yet evermore a grace for you.

The Difference

Although I have not seen you in quite a while,
emotions about you still rise and fall, undulating the same.
The difference is that I have not had a reason to smile,
for even the notions of missing you do remain ever so cruel.
The difference between my foolishness and my being a fool
was that I cared not for useless excuses yet found everything else to blame.

The pain of so many tear drops,
it seems that this rain never stops,
yet I will not be long in my sorrow,
after today, it will be gone before the dawn of tomorrow.

Although I have not heard from you in quite a while,
memories about you still ebb and flow, undulating the same.
The difference is that I have been given every occasion to smile,
for even if the concept of a forgiving heart is so inconceivable.
The difference that is now forgotten by all that is unbelievable
is also the choice that has remembered to do away with all of the shame.

Impatient tears pouring into deep oceans,
these become like a weight sinking within the waters of the great blue.
Shall I go there and try to retrieve sweet notions,
only to discover that those have been lost thru-out the cold depths of the untrue?

The 'I' of the Storm

How long will I live myself ever in a dream,
dying within the charms of a prefabricated fantasy?
Surely these things are never at all what they seem,
for myself and I perceive them no longer to be the sincerest actuality.

For then where is that which should assemble my certain future
when all I do is behold the animosity of the not too distant past?
For then there is that which does resemble my foolish human nature,
again and helplessly again…
when all I do is unfold and receive the enmity between it's varying contrast.

How long will I give myself over to a scheme,
sighing thru-out the arms of a premeditated misery?
Purely those things are never at all what they redeem,
for myself and I believe them no longer to be the securest factuality.

For then where is that which should be the security of my existence
when all I do is behold the inconsequence of my breath's ailing gasp?
For then there is that which would be the impurity of my resistance,
again and hopelessly again…
when all I do is unfold and achieve the indifference of my spirit's failing grasp.

The Present Gift of a Future Past
The Day After the Night Before Last

"...Follow through,
for today is the only way
to render tomorrow true.
So follow through."

α

A factuality so precisely exact…
for my very body and soul You do fill
with the depths of an ocean of such pure anticipation;
yes, the stealth of a mystery concealed
within which all memories of my sorrows last are so sweetly erased.

Ω

An actuality so concisely intact…
for my very spirit and mind You do still
with the breaths of a notion of such sure articulation;
know, the wealth of a secrecy revealed
thru-out which all miseries of my morrows last are completely replaced.

The World

When the world has taken one within it's grips
it is then that, by choice, one has become unevenly yoked.
Yet how the Word comes forth from another's lips
to break the hold of the one who has become spiritually choked.

If my conversations with you have meant anything
then I shall indeed honour what we together have agreed upon.
For my discussions with you have meant everything
in that they have freed and shed light about the truth of the dawn.

This Sorrow

A scent of your perfume
while I look at pictures of you;
sorrow is in full bloom
like a field of flowers that are blue.

So many memories,
I am sure that they haunt you too.
So many miseries,
I am sure that they want you too.

Once it was so sweet,
our love was like flowing ways of milk and honey.
Once it was complete,
our life was like knowing days so warm and sunny.

Contemplating the things of yesterday,
understanding the things of tomorrow;
presently In Absentia there remains no other way
for both you and I to be delivered from this sorrow.

Except within and thru-out the shining light
of the One Who has risen from the darkness of the night.

Thrice the Gist

α

While unfixed amidst the divided loyalty
of knowing all that is day from all that is night,
how could my mission's well being hope to find meaning
when my very heart and mind have become too scared to be afraid?
Permit me to once again understand the gist of what the quiet minority proclaims:
"For everyone's part so kind there could never be such a thing as instant maturity!"

Ω

While unfixed amidst the presided royalty
of knowing all that is dark from all that is light,
how could my vision's good seeing wish for lost dreaming
when my very soul and spirit have become too late to be delayed?
Permit me to twice again comprehend the gist of what the quiet minority proclaims:
"For everyone's goal so secret there could ever be such a thing as distant obscurity!"

Truth for You

My dear, you do not ever have to lie
and then proclaim that you are truthfully fine…
when your heart is clearly otherwise.
For is you so desire to understand me,
again comprehend me that you are purely free to know…
above and beyond all that is compromise.

Amidst the thorn of the flower and the weed,
as life's many failures taken oft times only seems to painfully succeed,
whether it is within a dire want and it's need,
surely love's plenty successes given always only deems to joyfully proceed.

My sweet, you do not ever have to sigh
and then exclaim that you are faithfully mine…
when your soul clearly is otherwise.
For if you so aspire to truly leave me,
again do believe me that you are surely free to go…
above and beyond all that is compromise.

Amidst the scorn of the soil and the seed,
as another's plowshare shall oft times cause the modest one to bleed,
whether it is thru-out a mire toil and it's feed,
purely another's wheat tare shall never cause the honest one to greed.

Ψ | mere observations

COLLECTION THREE
EupheMystic

A Graceful Figure*

A Reflection of Perfection

A Song Unknown*

All That Which Stars Construct*

Denial*

Depth Perception

Estranged

For All Eternity*

Here

Introductions*

Knowledge*

So Read

That Side of Heaven*

This Side of Heaven

The Four Winds*

Wish

Wisdom*

Your Person - For the Record*

Zero Visibility

Interactive Poem

mere observations | Ψ

A Graceful Figure

α

Yes, purely within my mean time desired
I spaciously think about all of the perfected dimensions of you.
For as all things do come unto a grinding halt,
every conception of your figure defined becomes inevitably true.

Wondrously the sorrows of the past, present, and future
are erased within the transcendent twinkling of a blinking eye.
For then combined with the embodiment of your truthful mind,
the beautiful heart of your graceful essence continually accepts my person.

Ω

Yes, surely within my dream time admired
I graciously feel about all of the respected devotions of you.
For as all things do come unto a winding fault,
every perception of your figure refined becomes indubitably new.

Splendrously the morrows of last resent of nature
are replaced thru-out the resplendent inkling of a winking sigh.
For then entwined with the enlightenment of your faithful kind,
the beautiful soul of your graceful presence perpetually protects my person.

A Reflection of Perfection

Just the reflection of you is the perfect image;
flawless visions of you are all that I can see.
For the perfection of you is a succinct visage;
faultless places with you is where I want To Be.

The places in the sky where you call home,
where eagles cry a sigh of perpetual relief.
The spaces in the night where you do roam,
where angels fly so high in continual belief.

A Song Unknown

α

This is a song unknown
yet it is sung by so many,
for those who are alone
sing it because they are empty.

Like a person with a featureless face
in the mirror there is a reflection I do not recognize.
Like a person with a futureless trace
amidst terror there is a perfection I can not emphasize.

Ω

That is a song unknown
yet it is played by so many,
for those who live alone
play it because they are plenty.

Like a person with a featureless place
in the mirror there is an image I no longer recognize.
Like a person with a futureless space
amidst horror there is a visage I no longer empathize.

All That Which Stars Construct

α *The Universe Beholding:*
While meditating a mourning dew
amidst the intricacy of each simplicity,
I eternally arrived with the surely complete
yet overcoming "Take My Hand" realization
that the actuality of the wondrous unity
of our bodies and souls preciously combined
are meant to understand the illumination
of **Life News**' one and only truthful revelation.

Do permit me to see the universe
thru-out the insight of your eyes tonight.
For your dreams and visions **Life New** revealed
are that which transcend the objects of mere symmetry perfected.
A supernatural definition of the twinkling stars
which unquestionably shine so exceptionally bright,
that to behold the flawlessness of their arranged configuration
is to comprehend the mystery wrapped within the riddle of everything shown.

Ω *The One-Disperse Unfolding:*
While contemplating a storming blue
amidst the delicacy of each complexity,
I eternally departed with the purely discrete
yet undergoing "Give My Hand" recognition
that the factuality of the splendrous entity
of our spirits and hearts graciously entwined
are meant to understand the communication
of **Love Trues**' one and only faithful explanation.

Do permit me to see the one-disperse
thru-out the foresight of your skies to light.
For your themes and missions for **Love True** concealed
are that which transcend the subjects of mere sympathy respected.
A metaphysical observation of the sparkling stars
which unanswerably shine so phenomenally right,
that to unfold the faultlessness of their estranged interpretation
is to comprehend the secrecy trapped within the middle of everything known.

Denial

α
I perish the thought of this emotion: You.
Yet cherish the essence of that conception: Us.
For then the truth of my thoughts and feelings sought true
to disclose what our time and space now concealed: Loneliness.

Ω
I won't acknowledge the persistence of this devotion: You.
Yet will encourage the presence of that perception: Us.
For then the faith of my thoughts and feelings sought new
to enclose what our date and place here revealed: Loveliness.

Depth Perception

Yes, I am overcome by the mere glance of your acute eyes,
with a fleeting look you see thru to depths of my soul.
Truly your very heart can discern another's undetected lies,
for the subtleness of the other's deceit is not hidden from it's goal.

Their ulterior motives are as plain as the day's light,
for every shifting shadow's transparency is brightly illuminated.
Where interior routines, although pitch black as night,
shine the spectrum of every colourful consciences' guilt insinuated.

Estranged

Listen and sojourn with me.
I can no longer talk with you
because of our so called differences
between all that is love and happiness.

Whisper and discern with me.
I can no longer walk with you
because of our so named consequences
amidst all that is life and loneliness.

Listen and sojourn with me.
I can no longer converse with you
because of our so called differences
between all that is hate and mystery.

Whisper and discern with me.
I can no longer traverse with you
because of our so named consequences
amidst all that is fate and destiny.

mere observations

For All Eternity

α

Yes, when my vision has become obscured
you define me to see what it is I am to see.
For your eyes contain salving incense
which purely does fill my bowl to over flowing:

A precious sight amidst all the illness around me
that I so stronger humble myself within your protection.
With all that is the spirit of my person's very heart,
I am thankful! that your loving grace abides for all eternity.

Ω

Yes, when my mission has become absurd
you refine me to be what it is I am to be.
For your sighs explain the solving essence
which surely does will my soul to ever knowing.

A gracious light amidst all the darkness around me
that I no longer stumble myself thru-out your direction.
Thru all that is the body of my person's every part,
I am grateful that your living love so guides for all eternity.

Here

While being driven by one thought
I did crash into a wall of emotion.
Your affection is all that I ever sought,
your attention is all that is my devotion.

There is just something about you: who are you?
There is just something within you: what are you?
There is just something around you: where are you?
There is just something thru-out you: why are you…
here?

Introductions

α

I wish to meet you
and tell you how I feel,
for all that is inside
I can no longer conceal.

Fulfill my conception,
bring my wish to fruition,
for preciously you are the only one
who can turn four plus three into seven.

Ω

I dream to greet you
and show you what is real,
for all that is outside
I must now truly reveal.

Bestill my perception,
take my dreams intuition,
for graciously you are the only one
who can turn the earth free into heaven.

Knowledge

α

With the good love of your knowledge so sweetly
you perpetually soothe my existence so tough.
For then satisfied, my very heart feels truly youthful
and emotions once scarred come and go so easily.

Ω

With the good life of your knowledge so neatly
you continually smooth my persistence so rough.
For then gratified, my every part thinks truly truthful
and devotions once hard ebb and flow ever so readily.

So Read

Yes, with just one look
your eyes do preciously speak in volumes.
So read like a book
your sighs say more than what one word presumes.

Yes, with just one glance
your eyes do graciously talk in mysteries.
So read like a chance
your sighs do more than what one deed remedies.

mere observations | Ψ

That Side of Heaven

Enter: EupheMystic
"Yes, that side of heaven,
so far away, apart from you.
Four plus three is seven,
so now today, my heart for you."

α

Elongated shadows parade about me
as I hear my loneliness knocking at the front door.
Eyes peer into the window of my stronghold
winking at me to open the concept that less is more.

While I hang my head in shame
silent voices present themselves hurriedly and loud.
Temptation says it's okay to play the game
if only I would come out from behind my cloud of gloom.

Ω

Serenaded sorrows charade around me
as I hear my aloneness knocking on the back door.
Sighs sneer into the window of my weak hold
waving at me to unlock the precept that rich is poor.

While I bang my dread in shame
quiet choices present themselves worriedly and proud.
Temptation says it's okay to stay the same
if only I would come out from behind my shroud of doom.

Exit: EupheMystic
"Goodbye, farewell."

This Side of Heaven

Enter: EupheMystic
"Yes, this side of heaven,
so far away, apart from you.
Four plus three is seven,
so now today, my heart for you."

It does me good to know you are doing well
and not just getting by or just doing okay.
Maybe we will get to see each other, who can tell?
All I hope is that it shall be someday.

Yes, this side of heaven,
I am doing fine, more than alright.
Just as four plus three is seven,
I wish you could be here tonight.

It does me well to know you are doing good
and not just falling down or just doing cliche.
Maybe we will get to see each other, wish we would.
All I pray is that it shall be one day.

Yes, this side of heaven,
I am doing alright, more than fine.
Just like the news at eleven,
I dream you could be truly mine.

Exit: EupheMystic
"Goodbye, farewell."

mere observations | Ψ

The Four Winds

α

Yes, you possess the most delicate touch;
it is comparable to the North wind as such.
Know, you possess that most intricate kiss;
it is comparable to the East wind like this.

Ω

Yes, you possess the most intimate touch;
it is comparable to the West wind as much.
Know, you possess the most exquisite kiss;
it is comparable to the South wind like bliss.

Wish

Preciously as the sun rises in the East
while I stand amidst the winds of the North,
understand that I could never wish you the least,
for only concerned blessings from my lips truly come forth.

Graciously as the sun sets in the West
while I stand amidst the winds of the South,
comprehend that I would always wish you the best,
for only discerned prayers go from the tongue of my mouth.

Wisdom

α

Wisdom, she illuminated my shadows
as she whispered to me aloud.
Forever times space and eternity my dearest
clear and how I do wondrously need to desire Thee.

Ω

Wisdom, she eliminated my sorrows
as she humbled me once so proud.
Forever times grace and eternity my nearest
Here and Now I do splendrously want to acquire Thee.

Ψ | mere observations

Your Person - For the Record

α

Yes, thoughts of you
fill the inside of my very heart,
indeed an emotion so true
that it can no longer hide within my very soul.

Yes, estrangement flees
the dark sight of all earthly loneliness,
as I do think and feel
about the admiration that I have for your person.

Ω

Yes, thoughts of you
will the outside of my every part,
indeed a devotion so new
that it can no longer reside thru-out my every goal.

Yes, arrangement frees
the stark light of all heavenly loveliness,
as I do see what's real
about the inspiration that I have from your person.

mere observations | Ψ

Zero Visibility

Why are you not free?
Why can't you just Be?
A mystery to me…
I wish you could see…

Understand that I am just trying to be your friend;
but maybe at the moment that is not what you are looking for.
Yet from the sour beginning unto the bitterness of the end
you comprehend that minus less is less equals plus more is more.

The intelligence of you I would dare not try to insult;
people playing their games to a "T" yet you are way too smart.
The foolishness of my emotions no longer do I consult
because you welcome all that comes from an honest heart.

With the key inserted please know my door is always open;
but do permit me to question why your person is always closed.
Like the melting metaphor of the north pole being frozen
to the wilderness-like desert elements of you, I am exposed.

Ψ | mere observations

COLLECTION FOUR
Dovetale of Dei Versatile Ink

A Quiescence's Soliloquy

An Article of Eminence

Another Day, Another Forever

As Yet Untitled - Act One, Scene One

As Yet Untitled - Act One, Scene Two

As Yet Untitled - Act Two, Scene One

As Yet Untitled - Act Two, Scene Two

Being…Itself

Bring Me Take Me

Butterfly*

Chamber of the Soul*

Coffee Shoppes Galore

Common Courtesy

Descending*

Elephant Shoes and Upside Down Smiles

Fidus Achates - Friend

Forever Moments

From Life New and it's Pain Unto Love True and it's Rain

Hope Against Hope

I Am That I Am*

I Become Alive For You*

I Do… So True*

Keeping Six Upon Seven*

Love Life Like Wise*

Melancholia

Meta 4 U

Mind and Heart

One Plus One*

Parallel

Perseverance

Plenty Blue

Said and Done

Sew it Seems

Sweet - All That Is Your Being*

Sweetest Debutante*

Thesauros - Treasure

Twilight

Uni Versus*

When Within Without Olive U

Why?

Without You x19

Wrong Writes

ΧΡΙΣΤΟΕ

Years of Grace: Upon Earth as it is in Heaven

Yes, Know One

Interactive Poem

mere observations | Ψ

A Quiescence's Soliloquy

Enter: Dovetale
"Loneliness of all that is Self.
When I am all alone,
when I am on my own,
it is so difficult to see anything else."

Your **Love True** presented a gift unto my lonely being,
a supernatural vision of **Life New** filled with such beautiful sentiments.
Sights of refined voice's speechlessness so worth seeing
that mine eyes once blind spoke volumes of such truthful commitments.

For just to merely conceive that I am kissing your sweet lips,
the notion that I do possess the soft warmth for your finger tips.
And all that which explains my heart and soul's absolute happiness
purely ascends thru-out the highest heights of the mountain of paradise.

Understand the dialects of this heavenly body language,
where one's objective movement becomes the only accepted form of expression.
Comprehend that these transcend earthly wisdom and knowledge,
a motive's improvement becomes the only respected mode of communication.

Yet just to clearly perceive that I am missing your smooth quips,
the motion when I do caress the symmetry of your curved hips.
And all that which contains my spirit and mind's ultimate loneliness,
surely descends within the deepest depths of the valley of such a cruel device.

Exit: Dovetale
Contemplating truth sincerely amidst the setting of the sun.
Meditating upon the warmth of the rising of next dawn.

An Article of Eminence

Time graciously spent alone with you,
yet it is Now that every dream is made a definite reality.
Space preciously shall condone the two,
for it is Here that every theme is beyond an infinite fantasy.

Just as an object is to it's lesson's dynamic,
I desire to understand the radiant energy which exists within your sweet love.
Amidst the knowledge of a heart so kinetic,
I implore the motions of your intimate kind to push and become all that is a gentle shove.

One moment purely shared alone with you,
yes it is Then that every wish is made a definite possibility.
The present surely shall condone the true,
for it is There that every hope is above an infinite probability.

Just as a subject is to it's person's polemic,
I aspire to comprehend the brilliant synergy which persists thru-out your dear love.
Amidst the wisdom of a spirit so prophetic,
I adore the notions of your intricate mind that go with the peace of a descending dove.

Another Day, Another Forever

The warmth of a bright summer day
possesses absolutely no meaning unto me
if I cannot save and spend it luxuriously with you.
For I desire all that is your love so sweetly
to fill the emptiness within my person until the passing of the night.
Yes, I require all that is your life completely
to truthfully understand that you are indeed all I shall care for evermore.

Within the miraculous Love True
of all that is your victorious Life New,
every day is a truthful day as such,
yes…one of all that which shall be many.

Never could there ever be another way
for me to express all that I wish your heart to see
except to say that this reality is all that I dream to do.
For I desire all that is your love preciously
to still the loneliness thru-out my being until the coming of the light.
Yes, I require all that is your life graciously
to faithfully comprehend that you are in fact all I shall share with and adore.

Thru-out the wondrous Love True
of all that is your glorious Life New,
every way is a faithful way as much,
yes…one of all that which shall be plenty.

As Yet Untitled - Act One, Scene One

Enter: Dovetale
Reclining upon the shoreline of the blue sea of tranquillity,
discerning the spectral setting of the sun amidst it's serenity.

Your Love True permits my person to forget the foolishness of the past
and remember truly all that exists within the pricelessness of the present.
For you permit my mission's being to do away with cruel regret from first to last
and surrender to all that persists thru-out the vicelessness of the moment.

My heart wishes you to submerge yourself
and bathe every illustration within the clarity of this acknowledgement,
for I shall tell you ever so softly all that I have aspired to do.
My soul dreams for you to immerse yourself
and wash every demonstration thru-out the purity of this encouragement,
for I shall show you ever so smoothly all that I have desired to do.

Your Life New comforts my person when I feel that I am so very alone
and ultimately respects everything within this realm which has become unconditional.
For you support my vision's seeing when I think that I am so on my own
and absolutely accept nothing thru-out that circle which has become inconsequential.

My mind needs you to esteem yourself
that I may be able to confess honourably all of these notions in fact,
for your impressions concealed are a treasure's immensity which I have aspired to find.
My spirit wants you to redeem yourself
that I may be able to express admirably all of these motions intact,
for your perfections revealed are a pleasure's intensity which I have desired so kind.

Exit: Dovetale
Departing into a western horizon as the deep blue tide evenly tempers.
Recognizing that the ebb and flow of what we think and feel is universal.

mere observations | Ψ

As Yet Untitled - Act One, Scene Two

Enter: Dovetale
"Wherever you are, I will always love you.
Whether near or far, I still always live you."

My dearest, everything that your heart sweetly desires,
these shall I do, for dreams mine spirit deeply admires.
More than a warm embrace, more than a superficial kiss,
understand truly that your command is my soul's every wish.

Just like raindrops upon one's soil,
your being permeates my each and every notion;
for you encapture the embodiment of all that I have ever thought.
Just like teardrops upon one's toil,
your person saturates my each and every emotion;
for you enrapture the enlightenment of all that I have ever sought.

My nearest, just as four plus three is always invariably seven,
comprehend that it is your **Love True** which does send me unto heaven.
For what shall it mean to be without your **Life New** so well,
but to dwell within and thru-out the deepest regions of all that is hell.

Just as the absence of midnight is twilight,
your presence penetrates my each and every intention;
for you possess the possibility that all things are indeed attainable.
Just as the substance of insight is so right,
your essence infiltrates my each and every ambition;
for your profess the probability that all things are in fact obtainable.

Exit: Dovetale
Considering past notions of the potentiality of Future antiquity.
Understanding last motions of the plausibility of Space and Timelessness.

As Yet Untitled - Act Two, Scene One

Enter: Dovetale
"If unto my loneliness
there remains no companion,
then unto your loveliness
there explains no comparison."

Most unreservedly
I do want all that is you.
Just like a barren land desires rain
to replenish it so that it may survive morrow's last.

As yet to be known so modest and true,
I do wish to understand the complete notions of you;
the perfected conception that defines your very heart and mind.
The deepest of all emotion searching the depth of your every part so kind.

Most undeservedly
I do need all that is you.
Just like a bitter man requires pain
to remind him how he truly endured sorrows past.

As yet to be shown so modest and new,
I do hope to comprehend the discrete actions of you;
the respected perception that refines your very soul and spirit.
The sweetest of all devotion purging the breadth of your every goal so secret.

Exit: Dovetale
"And when I am happy that I am sad,
realize that it does me well
to meditate upon the fact that you are there.
And when I am angry that I am glad,
recognize that it does me good
to contemplate upon the act that you do care."

mere observations | Ψ

As Yet Untitled - Act Two, Scene Two

Enter: Dovetale
Sitting atop the highest peak on the mountain of comprehension.
Meditating the height, width, depth, and length of the cosmos.

Immediately when your astute conceptions
gracefully inspire all that constitutes my person,
their beautiful possibilities truthfully fulfills
it's dimensions with the warmth of all that is the probability of daylight.
For then the clarity of your acute perceptions
liberates my being from what institutes it's prison.
There your mystical essence faithfully bestills
all of the wistful queries which I consider during the hours of midnight.

For the question asked is this: Just what is it like to truly miss you?
But to fathom within my possession the worthlessness of all that is sure loneliness.
For the answer masked is this: Just what is it like to truly kiss you?
But to value thru-out my confession the pricelessness of all that is pure loveliness.

How then I hope and wish
that you and your wondrous devotions were aware of Here.
So that I may be able to tell you within speechlessness
all that the composition of my very heart and mind has thought.
For now I dream and wish
that you and your splendrous emotions were there ever near,
so that I may be able to show you thru-out wordlessness
all that the disposition of my every part so kind has sought.

For if I have spoken eloquently on the unity of time and space
it is because I no longer desire to be within the factuality of your absence.
For if I have written excellently on the harmony of date and place
it is because I so stronger require to be thru-out the actuality of your presence.

Exit: Dovetale
Stirring the clear crystalline waters
of the deepest fountain of understanding.
Wondering if the rippling reflections
shall ever see more than just the memory of your image.

Being…Itself

As situations do exchange
and circumstances rearrange
yet there is one factuality that I have always known:
it is the pure morality of the fact that my love for you defines everlasting.

The reality of this constantly remembers each and every thing
that my mind should have forgotten the existence of so long ago.
Yet within the confusion of each and every age I do still truthfully know
that my heart clearly does understand that I shall always love you above
being…itself.

As visitations do exchange
and consequences new estrange
yet there is one actuality that I have always shown:
it is the immortality of the act that my love for you refines everlasting.

The identity of this instantly surrenders each and every thing
that my soul would have forsaken the persistence of so long ago.
Yet thru-out the commotion of each and every stage I do still faithfully show
that my spirit dearly does comprehend that I shall always love you beyond
being…itself.

mere observations | Ψ

Bring Me Take Me

Possess me and hold me,
bring me into your image.
Caress me and mould me,
take me into your visage.

If I should hide,
would you desire to find me?
If I should inside,
would you still act kindly?

Bring me out with your inspiration.
Bring me out with your compassion.
Bring me out with your admiration.
Bring me out with your devotion.

And if I should hide where again,
please I do request you to find me.
And if I would hide there again,
permit me to leave my past behind me.

Take me in with your adoration.
Take me in with your compassion.
Take me in with your aspiration.
Take me in with your emotion.

Butterfly

α

Delicately please sweet butterfly
do tell me why many a thoughts flutter
try to understand amidst an angel's silent majority
how it is the glamour of your wings could be as soft as silk.

Ω

Intricately please sweet butterfly
do show me why plenty a thoughts clutter
try to comprehend amidst all heaven's quiet minority
why is it the splendor of your wings could be as smooth as milk.

mere observations | Ψ

Chamber of the Soul
For Kamara

α

When your inescapable presence
graces the measure of the room,
the pleasant elegance of you fills it
from the floor to the height of it's ceiling dimension.
For then the mystery of your nearness
replaces the obscurity of my impeding gloom
with a vision which permits the authentic revelation
of my being's inspiration to maintain a healthy emotion.

As the promise of my very heart revealed
does long to belong with the person that is you,
understand that the whole of my every part enclosed
is made pure within the attitude of redeemed motivation.
For these words of honour spoken desire
to tell you what should be said so true,
again with an honesty that respects the factuality,
patience is the quality needed to soothe your hesitation.

Ω

When your inevitable absence
traces the pleasure of the room,
the fragrant excellence of you stills it
from the door to the might of it's sealing conclusion.
For then the memory of your dearness
erases the absurdity of my transcending doom
with a mission which permits the angelic elevation
of my being's admiration to sustain a wealthy devotion.

As the premise of my very mind concealed
does yearn to discern with the person that is you,
comprehend that the soul of my every kind disclosed
is made sure thru-out the gratitude of esteemed captivation.
For those deeds of valour written aspire
to show you what should be done so new,
again with a modesty that accepts the actuality
silence is the quantity heeded to smooth your apprehension.

Coffee Shoppes Galore

Seeing coffee shoppes galore,
how all of these do remind me of you.
Reminders from a coffee parlour,
sincerely odd my friend, but so true.

For quite sure the odyssey is this,
that such a common everyday place
would make me wish for your sweet kiss
and let me wonder about your warm embrace.

mere observations | Ψ

Common Courtesy

You and I are one and the same,
concealing no guilt, arrogance, or shame.
For we give within a common courtesy
and live thru-out the freedom of this liberty.

You and I possess a sincere understanding,
an unspoken agreement that shall never fail.
For we comprehend that **Love True** is undemanding,
the gifts and fruit of the spiritual life shall always prevail.

You and I appreciate all things which are faithful,
although about some things we may agree to disagree.
For we know this is the only way to remain truthful,
there is never another means to explain how to be truly free.

You and I are one and the same,
revealing no worry, ignorance, or blame.
For we care within a common courtesy
and share thru-out the wisdom of that clarity.

You and I transcend each and every circumstance,
what is of the utmost concern is all that we are.
For **Life New** surpasses each and every encumbrance,
even if the hurtful wounds should leave a disfiguring scar.

You and I embody the spirit of this divine fact:
the notion of true compassion, free of the obscure emotion, is a genuine act.
More than just a concept or a precept intact:
forgiveness is a decision, whose unsigned volition, is an unconditional contract.

Descending

α

Yes, just like intricate words
descending upon the callousness of deaf ears,
mine are comparable to warm
teardrops descending upon the coldness of your very heart.

Ω

Yes, just like delicate birds
descending upon the sharpness of leaf shears,
it is unbearable to form
teardrops descending upon the boldness of your every part.

mere observations | Ψ

Elephant Shoes and Upside Down Smiles

I love you…
I so would enjoy early morning walks with you in the park.
I need you…
all of you and the ad lib conversations.
I want you…
all of you and these sweet improvisations.
I adore you…
to know the truth of those talks from sunrise until after dark.

4 Olive U I wear elephant shoes and an upside down smile.
Scarlet Red with the blues, Crimson Purple weeps all the while.

I love you…
as you and I journey to the ideal knowledge of one another.
I need you…
there could never be a higher wisdom to understand.
I want you…
there could never be a deeper freedom to comprehend.
I adore you…
the streams of life and the springs of love which flow unto each other.

4 Olive U I wear elephant shoes and an upside down smile.
Scarlet Red with the blues, Crimson Purple weeps all the while.

Grace my heart with your life's presence,
permit my soul to be enraptured within the shift of this moment.
For There and Then, there will be no conception of Dates and Places past,
only the sincere realization of all that sweetly exists Here and Now.

Bless my mind with your love's essence,
permit my spirit to be enraptured thru-out the gift of that Present.
For where and again, there will be no perception of Times and Spaces last,
only the honest recognition of all that deeply consists of promise's vow.

Fidus Achates - Friend

Enter: Dovetale
"You have inspired me
so I have admired thee.
Like a glance is also a touch,
permit me to say just how much."

Each and every devotion
that your contemplating mind
may have so preciously thought,
this is therefore the sweetest conception.

You are beautifully designed,
for you are wonderfully defined.
Of all the ideas that my being has ever sought,
amidst my loneliness you are my glorious inspiration.

Each and every emotion
that your mediating heart
may have so graciously felt,
this is wherefore the deepest perception.

Your elegance is a refined work of art,
for your eloquence silently speaks of it's every part.
As the misery of my loneliness begins to melt,
amidst my aloneness you are my victorious admiration.

Exit: Dovetale
"A first glance at a second chance
is to view each and every circumstance,
where I see your eyes speak volumes
without the use of what a mere word presumes."

mere observations | Ψ

Forever Moments

When my presence is ever close to you
it is then that my anticipation inspires me.
Sweetest moments ever graciously true
that within utmost purity my very heart becomes free.

For all the excellent things you purely do
please understand that I love these things every day so new.
For all of the wondrous things you surely do to me
could never compare thru-out my every part with all that comes to be.

Like a warm sun shower in June
or a cool snow flurry in July.
Like loneliness under a cherry moon
or loveliness filling an endless supply.

When my absence is ever far from you
it is then that my infatuation admires thee.
Dearest moments ever preciously true
that within foremost clarity my very mind becomes free.

For all of the elegant things you purely do
please comprehend that I live those things every way so new.
For all the splendrous things you surely do to me
could never despair thru-out my every kind with all that comes to be.

Like a hot summer breeze in August
or a cold winter freeze in September.
Like possessing faith where there is only chosen mistrust
or confessing truth where there is lonely frozen what miseries remember.

From Life New and it's Pain
Unto Love True and it's Rain

Yes, **Life New** and the pain
of it's reasons
are always ebbing and flowing.
As **Love True** and the rain
of it's seasons
are always reaping and sowing.

Understand that my devotion to you will always be
like knowledge knowing
that there is a difference between the consequence
of dying and growing.
Know, if for the future of yesterday there shall be
no past for tomorrow,
comprehend that today your perfection shall see me
thru all that is my sorrow.

Hope Against Hope

To be caught dead within the glance
of the cool unavoidability of your presence
is to witness the inseparable essence
of a precious Time and Space's perfected moment.
For the existence of theses are filled
with the brilliant harmony of wondrous notions
which long to eternally encapture the instance
between all that has become the reality of There and Then.

As I hope that the sweet spirit
of your mind will purely understand
and see that the admiration of your wishes
are the deepest captivation of my person's every command.
Yes I hope that the dear secret
of your kind will greet love's open hand
and see that the aspiration of our kisses
are the sweetest fascination of my being's every demand.

To be sought thru out the chance
of the cruel inevitability of your absence
is to possess the indescribable substance
of a gracious Date and Place's respected event.
For the consistence of those are willed
by the elegant unity of splendrous motions
which yearn to eternally enrapture the distance
between all that has become the finality of Where and When.

As I hope that the very heart
of your soul will surely comprehend
and see that the objects of your dreams esteemed
are in fact the fulfillment of mine realizing that you are a Godsend.
Yes, I hope that the every part
of your whole will greet life's only friend
and see that the subjects of your themes redeemed
are intact and the stillness of mine recognize that you are heaven sent.

Ψ | mere observations

I am That I am

α

And when I am happy that I am sad,
by your very heart and mind
are the intentions of mine weighed,
for by your very soul and spirit
are the ambitions of mine measured.
How stronger do I precisely love you?
And when my earthly death has been fulfilled,
please understand my dearest…
how could I ever amount the strength of these ways?

Ω

And when I am angry that I am glad,
by your every part so kind
is the loneliness of mine stayed,
for by your every goal so secret
is the aloneness of mine treasured.
How longer shall I graciously live you?
And when my worldly breath has been stilled,
please comprehend my nearest…
how could I ever account the length of those days?

mere observations | Ψ

I Become Alive for You

α
Within the dead of the night
I become alive and willed by a desire for you,
for it is here and when
I become captivated with a new passion for you.

Ω
Thru-out the thread of this light
I become alive and filled by a blue fire for you,
for it is near and then
I become stimulated with a true notion for you.

I Do... So True

α

Not a day passes by
when I do not think of you,
for to deny this fact would be to imply
the truth which resides before the lie.
For when I proclaim I do not love you,
purely your very heart and mind understands that I do…
so true.

Ω

Not a night passes by
when I do not dream of you,
for to deny this act would be to imply
the truth which presides after the lie.
For when I exclaim I do not live for you,
surely your every part so kind comprehends that I do…
so true.

mere observations | Ψ

Keeping Six Upon Seven

Enter: Sir Dovetale
Sitting upon the vast edge of forever,
dreaming of sailing the sea of eternity.

α *Amidst the lies of a devil:*
When the voice of reason is silent
I do trust all that you have to say.
For without you there is no tomorrow
and there is no purpose for me to exist

Ω *Amidst the sighs of an angel:*
When the choice for treason is quiet
I do trust all that you have today.
For without you there is only sorrow
and there is no purpose for me to persist.

2u4u

Exit: Sir Dovetale
"The Real is the Rational
and the Rational is the Real!"

Ψ | mere observations

Love Life Like Wise

α *Love True Beholding:*
While accepting the deepest fixation
of a broken daydream's most intricate simplicity,
amidst the unwinding youth of my very heart and mind,
do permit me to kiss these meditations
which likewise ripple smoothly within your very soul and spirit.
For like an overflowing river gushing,
I desire to understand the pleasure's immensity
of caressing the essence of your thoughts, words, and deeds
as their inspiration cascades into the deeper mysteries of your existence.

Just as darkness flees
the inevitable presence of twilight
to fill and purely constitute
a morrow's unmixed absence of night,
the solace of your love true is like
the careful warmth of the rising sun
which glistens upon the diamond raindrops madly falling
until the storming thundershowers of the present noon duly subside.

Ω *Life New Unfolding*
While respecting the sweetest conviction
of a token esteem's most delicate complexity,
amidst the unbinding truth of my every part so kind,
do permit me to taste those contemplations
which likewise trickle sweetly thru-out your every goal so secret.
For like an ever knowing quiver rushing,
I aspire to comprehend the measure's intensity
of possessing the substance of your thoughts, wants, and needs
as their admiration parades unto the higher secrecies of your persistence.

Just as sadness frees
the unavoidable absence of twilight
to will and surely institute
a sorrow's unfixed presence of midnight,
the promise of your Life New is like
the prayerful strength of the setting one
which sparkles upon the diamond teardrops sadly calling
until the forming wonder-hours of the crescent moon truly preside.

mere observations | Ψ

Melancholia

Exit: Sir Dovetale's pre-meditation.
Upon the pinnacle of despair,
yes I do sit and patiently wait.
Mountainous view of disrepair,
yet I do watch and silently contemplate.

The summits are capped with ice and snow,
for these are the apexes of various sorrows and fears.
Cliffs of loneliness to understand and know,
amongst the amalgam of today's sadness and tears…

concealed.

Enter: Dovetale's post-contemplation.
Amidst all the pain,
I do behold You standing there.
For when sorrow falls like rain,
You shelter me with all that is Your love's care.

Taking me by the want of my hand
unto higher ground You safely lead the very heart of my soul.
Giving me what I need to understand
as Your Life New surpasses the comprehension of all circumstance's control.

Amidst all the strife,
I do behold You right by my side.
For You have not left my life,
but have strengthened me with the love that you provide.

Cherishing me as a good friend,
victoriously unto safety You have led the very mind of my spirit.
Nourishing me from beginning to end,
gloriously Your Love True is The Everlasting: the universe's mysterious secret…

revealed.

Ψ | mere observations

Meta 4 U

α
Just as subjects are for themes,
elaborate compositions written about thee
fill great encyclopedic volumes of reflection
which reside within the library of my very heart and mind.

Ω
Just as objects are for dreams,
eloquent expositions spoken about thee
will flawlessly paint pictures of perfection
which preside thru-out the gallery of my every part so kind.

Mind and Heart

Your mind is so sharp
just like a two-edged sword.
You do play me as a harp
with the beautiful music of your every word.
Permit me to graciously dwell
within the length of your notions for all days.

Your heart is so sweet
just like mixed honey and milk.
You do make me complete
with the wonderful tapestry of your very silk.
Permit me to preciously dwell
thru-out the strength of your motions for all ways.

Ψ | mere observations

One Plus One

α

While my appreciations exchange
and their appropriations rearrange
amidst no thoughts of sordid gain,
please accept as a fact that my only concern is for you.

For with just one word's eloquence
from the symmetric splendor of your soft lips,
and all that has become so sadly mistaken
emerges corrected as though it's fallacy had never existed.

Ω

While my sweet devotions exchange
and their sour emotions re-estrange
amidst no thoughts of morbid pain,
please respect as an act that my lonely sojourn is for you.

For with just one deed's elegance
from the majestic wonder of your smooth quips,
and all that has become so badly misgiven
converges perfected as though it's misery had never persisted.

Dovetale of Dei Versatile Ink

Parallel

Faithfully
your heart is so sweet
that I would die just to live
for all that you perceive to be your love.

Wondrously
your soul is so deep
that I have wished
to descend within your depths
with the gentleness of a landing dove.

Truthfully
your mind is so complete
that I would cry just to give
myself unto all that which you do conceive thereof.

Splendrously
your spirit is so high
that I have dreamed
to ascend thru-out your heights
with the momentum of a playful push coming to a shove.

Ψ | mere observations

Perseverance

Ultimately, this is not an easy road
that you and I have chosen to journey upon.
Many times it is just too hard to bear the load
when it only seems that this darkness will not turn into dawn.

Absolutely, there remains the one true hope
that you and I must endeavor to eternally agree upon.
For when our despair declares that we are unable to cope,
let us consider the voice of Him Who promises new strengths to carry on...
and on...
and on...

mere observations | Ψ

Plenty Blue

Yes, when I am within the presence of you
it purely seems that I just cannot truly be me.
Yet, when I am thru-out the absence of you
it surely deems that I just cannot truly be free.

So yes, within thru-out you
it is a match plenty blue.
Oh no, with or without you
it is a catch twenty two.

Ψ | mere observations

Said and Done

Enter: Dovetale
"What else could I say
except that which has not been said all before.
What else could I do
except that which has not been done all the more."

I am in love with your being's perfected beauty,
with the sweet essence which defines all that is your very heart.
I am in love with your person's respected duty,
with the dear substance which designs all that is your every part.

Yes, you are as delicately detailed as an untamed flower
whose spectrum of fragrance fills the universe's unending expanse called "the sky".
Like a kingdom intricately availed with majestic power,
your royal subjects are the loyal truth of it's courts which cast out the objects of the lie.

I am in love with your being's true sincerity,
with the nourishing fruit of your spirit's flourishing tree so fulfilling.
I am in love with your person's honest clarity,
that to die for you as my soul lives, it is prepared and has become so willing.

Know, your mind references every absolute notion thought,
like when a book of wisdom is written and placed within the library of your purest conceptions.
For your kind reverences every ultimate emotion wrought,
like when a scroll of poetic literature is spoken thru-out the gallery of your surest perceptions.

Exit: Sir Dovetale
"My words die for you
to resurrect that which has not been said all before;
my deeds live for you
to circumspect that which has not been done all the more.

Sew It Seems

How you and I did fall apart at the "seems"
within the true heart of the imagination of our dreams.
All of the blessings that we could not "sow"
thru-out all of the power that our aspirations did not know.

An enemy? Yes, the end result was disbelief,
for you and I did not choose to diffuse the fears.
A Friend? Know, the murderer and thief,
for you and I did not learn to discern: to refuse the tears.

What was our vision?
What was our purpose?
In sickness and in health
graciously there was **Life New** to live,
for this truthfully was our anointed promise,
yet…meaning still exists.

What was our mission?
What was our surplus?
In poverty and in wealth,
preciously there was **Love True** to give,
for that faithfully was our appointed solace,
yet…dreaming still persists.

Sweet - All That Is Your Being

α *Rest Assured My Dearest:*
Yes, purely when I am unadmired
it is then I truly drink of your being.
Sweet contemplations of you fill my soul
emotionally…
my very spirit wants to take all that is you so dear.

Ω *Best Assured My Nearest*
Yes, surely when I am unrequired
it is then I truly yearn for your being.
Sweet meditations for you still my whole
convincingly…
my every secret needs to taste all that is you so near.

Sweetest Debutante

α *The Haunting:*
Sweetest debutante
with all that is a memory's reflection,
my soul do you haunt
with all that is a mystery's perfection.

Above despair
and beyond pleasure,
permit me to truthfully imagine
the logical progression of what entails…
as yet to be known.

Ω *The Wanting:*
Sweetest debutante
with all that is a clarity's distinction,
your love do I want
with all that is a purity's exception.

Above compare
and beyond measure,
permit you to faithfully examine
the magical succession of what prevails…
as yet to be shown.

Ψ | mere observations

Thesauros - Treasure

Your mind is a pearl of wisdom;
for your **Life New** is invaluable like that of a precious jewel.
Your heart is a diamond of freedom;
for your **Love True** is incomparable like that of the Golden Rule.

Yes, you are the treasure of a smile so beautifully given;
the dearest admiration to all those who confess allegiance to thee in secret.
For you are the pleasure of a glance so wonderfully taken;
the sincerest inspiration to all those who profess observance of thee in spirit.

Know, you are the measure of a mystery so wrapped within a riddle;
the purest conception of all that is defined to explain your existence and truth.
For you are the erasure of the secrecy so trapped thru-out the middle;
the surest perception of all that is refined to contain your innocence and youth.

Twilight

I. Dawn Unto Light:
Within the waking charms of Orpheus,
yes, I do think of all that is your Life New daily.
For you are indeed my very heart's inspiration
that truly chases all the storm clouds of gloom away.
For to just remember the beautiful form of your grace again
I forget all of the loneliness and rejoice an eternity times ten.

II. Dusk Unto Night:
Thru-out the sleeping arms of Morpheus,
know, I do dream of all that is your Love True nightly.
For you are in fact my every part's admiration
which purely sends all the dark shrouds of doom astray.
For if by Divine Appointment we should see another moment's place and date
to forever rest in thee would be heaven's open door as our Father closes the gate.

III. Destiny...

Ψ | mere observations

Uni Versus
All things combined into One.

α *Amidst Loneliness Unfolding:*
As loneliness so motionlessly reveals
the temporary disposition of one's conceptions,
please do understand that the sum of my soul
and it's very heart enclosed has yearned for you for so long.
A length of fulfilling true admiration
for the grandeur of your resplendent notions
which abolish the webs of deceit encapturing
the creativity overcoming within the imagination of my mind's eye.

While questions account what measures
I would take to convince your recognition,
all of these acknowledgments wish to give the rest
of life's treasures thru-out the possibility of all that is you and I.
For here and now they desire to surely meet
the insightful spirit of our divine vision seeing,
the absolute contemplation upon all that could be known.
To be the There and Then factuality of all that should be you and I.

Ω *Amidst Loveliness Beholding:*
As loveliness so notionlessly conceals
the transitory constitution of one's perceptions,
please do comprehend that the sum of my whole
and it's every part disclosed has learned from you to be strong.
A strength of bestilling new fascination
for the splendor of your transcendent motions
which demolish the threads of conceit enrapturing
the objectivity undergoing within the examination of my kind's sigh.

While answers surmount what pressures
I would break to persuade your realization,
all of those encouragements hope to live the best
of love's pleasures thru-out the probability of all that is you and I.
For dearly how they aspire to purely greet
the delightful secret of our combined mission being,
the ultimate meditation upon all that could be shown.
To be the Where and When actuality of all that would be you and I.

When Within Without Olive U

And when I do miss your company just a little too much
my mind understands what it means to be alone within one and lonely.
Although from this conception I might be so absolutely forsaken,
yet still do I preciously accept the metaphysical essence which is all of you
so true.

And when I do kiss your mystery's trust and riddle as such
my heart comprehends what it means to be so sad without one and only.
Although unto this perception I might be so ultimately mistaken,
yet still do I graciously respect the super-mystical substance which is all of you
so true.

Why?

Why does the world keep on turning?
Is it not for the sake of the chosen few?
Why do these fires keep on burning?
Is it not for the life that is within you?

Why is the universe still in existence?
Is it not for the sake of the aforementioned elect?
Why does this disperse still in consistence?
Is it not for the reason that you are my choice, so very select?

Why does the earth keep on turning?
Is it not for the purpose that you and I may understand?
Why do those desires keep on yearning?
Is it not for the meaning that He has taken us by the hand?

Why is space and time still an actuality?
Is it not so that all may comprehend redemption in the present?
Why is grace and crime still a factuality?
Is it not because if you are late, He should not mark you absent?

mere observations | Ψ

Without You x19

Without you...
things have not been the same
without you...
life has become for me
without you...
just another empty exercise.

Without you...
when I go to sleep at night
without you...
I dream of you until the next light
without you...
the rising sun offers no comfort
without you...
for your sweet love was my only support
without you...
there is no trace left of your life at all
without you...
yet is it right when I hear your lonely voice call?

Without you...
things have been to blame
without you...
love has become for me
without you...
a consequence filled with lonely sighs.

Without you...
when I awake in the thunderous mourning
without you...
thoughts of you in mind are silently storming
without you...
the setting sun offers, to say the least, no rest
without you...
for loneliness follows suit from the East to the West
without you...
there is no place upon the face of the earth that I can run
without you...
to escape the everlasting fact that your sweet love is the only one...
for the all of me
yet I am still...
without you.

Wrong Writes

With your harsh piercing words,
yes, how your loveliness does slay me.
Milk and honey turned to curds,
know, how your loneliness does repay me.

With the frozen coldness of your heart
combined with the chosen darkness of your mind,
the denial of your boldness tears me apart,
for no other refusal to understand could be as unkind.

mere observations | Ψ

ΧΡΙΣΤΟΣ

Truthfully
your complete loving compassion
removes every shadow casting mountains of doubt.
As in it's great enlightenment,
there is no shifting variation, nor a dark lie.
For thru-out Your True Love's many sureties,
oh yes Heart of Hearts,
it is indeed the treasure of Your loving kindness' regeneration
that is so divinely precious unto the very essence of one and all.

Beautifully
this loving treasure has encaptured
purely my very hardened heart and soul.
To understand so dearly,
so deep within my being's innermost,
the existence of Your loving kindness made in justification,
spiritually is the freedom and comfort that I do so gloriously desire.
Selah.

Faithfully
Your sweet loving Companion
springs forth an everlasting fountain enroute.
It is a shower of refreshment,
living purification from the heights of the sky.
For thru-out Your New Life's many purities,
oh yes Soul of Souls,
it is indeed the pleasure of Your loving kindness' consummation
that is genuinely gracious unto the very substance of one and all.

Wonderfully
the loving pleasure has enraptured
surely my every forsaken part, whole.
To comprehend sincerely
so high above my being's outermost,
the consistence of Your loving tenderness laid in sanctification
universally in the wisdom and support that I do so victoriously require.
Selah.

Ψ | mere observations

Years of Grace:
Upon Earth as it is in Heaven

α Once Upon a Time and Space:
Upon the cusp of a love
that could again be so right,
the definition of you is sweetly
all that is a terrestrial push to a shove.

My dearest, do permit me to understand
all that is the future of your personal history,
yes, the intangible qualities which define for your mind,
all that is clarity of an esteemed notion's everlasting existence.

For within the unbroken continuity which so explains
all that is the given strength of my enlightened mission's being,
dwells also the immense curiosity that yearns like a cherubim to look into
all that is contemplated upon amidst the poetry of your thought's every want and need.

Ω Twice Upon a Date and Place:
Upon the wing of a dove
that would again be in flight,
the explanation of you is neatly
all that is a celestial pull from above.

My nearest, do permit me to comprehend
all that is the nature of your spiritual mystery,
yes, the invisible quantities which refine for your kind,
all that is the purity of a redeemed motion's everlasting persistence.

For thru-out the unspoken perpetuity which so sustains
all that is the taken length of my enbrightened vision's seeing,
dwells also the intense luminosity that burns like seraphim to look into
all that is meditated upon amidst the symmetry of your thought's every word and deed.

Yes, Know One

α

How beautiful you are.
How beautiful you are my dearest.
Your eyes are like doves.
Who would I eternally Be without you?

Yes, Know One.

Ω

How wonderful you are.
How wonderful you are my nearest.
You whom my soul loves.
What would I eternally Be without you?

Yes, Know One.

Ψ | mere observations

COLLECTION FIVE
StrataGem's Pearl of Wisdom

A Symmetry's Eloquence*

An Autumn Evening*

Check Mate

From a Diamond Tear Drop
Unto a Pearl of Wisdom

From Everlasting to Everlasting*

Grace At Your Table

Just*

One Two Another*

Parallel*

Persons Being*

Post Mortem for You*

Questions for You*

Spirit Level I
The Name of Inspiration*

Spirit Level II
The Name of Admiration*

Spirit Level III
The Name of Aspiration*

Spirit Level IV
The Name of Captivation*

Spirit Level V
The Name of Motivation*

Spirit Level VI
The Name of Fascination*

Spirit Level VII
The Name of Explanation*

Spirit Level VIII
The Name of Definition*

Spirit Level IX
The Name of Declaration*

Spirit Level X
The Name of Exploration*

Spirit Level XI
The Name of Demonstration*

Spirit Level XII
The Name of Realization*

Superficial Again*

That Which Transcends*

The Conclusion for Certain*

The One Who Came
and Went Undone*

The Truth Apart*

Thoughts of You*

True Love for You*

Undone No Longer*

Under The Sun*

Untitled for You*

With You*

Eaves Dropping
Upon Adam's Apple

Immortal Continuum

Interactive Poem

A Symmetry's Eloquence

α

While this very heart of mine
becomes a gesturing paradigm
when my mind cannot precisely define
all that the wants and needs these thoughts do wish to tell you.

Permit their admiration to understand the intimate ecstasy
which is eloquently contained within the gist of the depths of moonlit sigh.
For I do ponder on the setting of the sun as evensong
about the symmetric excellence of the perfection of your devotion that is willed
by pure logic.

Ω

While this every part of mine
becomes a pestering pantomime
when my kind cannot concisely design
all the words and deeds those thoughts do hope to show you.

Permit their adoration to comprehend the delicate secrecy
which is consequently sustained thru-out the midst of a sunlit sky.
For I do wonder on the rising of the sun as morning dawn
about the symmetric elegance of the dimension of your emotion that is filled
with sure magic.

Ψ | **mere observations**

An Autumn Evening

α Exit the Solar Spectrum of Light:
Essentially as deep as these thoughts are as wide my dearest,
purely I despite to show the entirety of your person just how I really feel,
for within the transcendent blinking of your beautiful eyes
the spectrum of light from the sun's shower cascades an eastern rainbow.
I wish to understand the depth of the many factual things
which do sail across the oceans of the deepest notions of your intelligence
while I bathe amidst the warm descent of the sun's disk
as it sets upon the clarion of your mind.

For if the presence of company still brings with it all that is so lonely,
here I will believe you indeed and proclaim that your very heart enclosed is not
so alone.
Yet if the existence which is defined as your tears are the only ones solely,
now I shall accept you in need and exclaim that your every part disclosed is
not on their own.

Ω Enter the Lunar Sanctum of Night:
Substantially as sweet as those thoughts are inside my nearest,
surely I aspire to know the sincerity of your being just so ideally real,
for thru-out the brilliant twinkling of the stars which are your eyes
the sanctum of night from the moon's hour parades a western shadow.
I dream to comprehend the breadth of the many actual things
which prevail en masse the quotients of the sweetest motions of your smooth elegance,
yet while I lay under the cool crescent for the moon's mist
as it rises upon the horizon of your kind.

For if the absence of misery still brings with it all that is so lonely,
there I will receive you in fact and declare that your very spirit concealed is not
so alone.
Yet if the persistence which is refined as your tears are the only ones solely,
then I shall respect you intact and so swear that your every secret revealed is
not on their own.

Check Mate

Just like a game of chess
I am pondering my next move.
From a strategy of loneliness
my love for you I cannot seem to prove.

To simply win this game of chess
there is only one last and final move.
To end the strategy of loneliness
just say these words and then it is proved:

I love you.

Ψ | mere observations

From a Diamond Tear Drop
Unto a Pearl of Wisdom

Regardless of what one may conceive to be real,
please do understand that with every day which has come
the strength of love for you that I would truly feel
could only be made stronger within the total of this sum.

Amidst such a flawless eloquence designed
of that which for eternity can never be further defined,
the poetic harmony of your gracious words and deeds combined
are quantified as existing above perfection thru-out my very heart and mind.

Regardless of what one may perceive to be hate,
please do comprehend that with every night which has gone
the length of time for you that I would truly wait
could only be made longer within the spectra of this dawn.

Amidst such a faultless elegance assigned
of that which for eternity can never be further refined,
the symmetric unity of your precious wants and needs entwined
are qualified as persisting beyond correction thru-out my every part so kind.

mere observations | Ψ

From Everlasting to Everlasting

α *Amidst a Recurring Theme:*
Yes, permit me to make an everlasting impression
and tell your person that my thoughts upon your precious elegance
are always of the foremost perfected conceptions
which desire no further definition to be esteemed an exceptional excellence.

For if daily worries should yet design my words and deeds
please do understand that the strength of my concern for your very heart and mind
remains all that is above and beyond a temporary worldly emotion
which is measured deeply by the inexplicable intentions of your very soul and spirit.

Ω *Amidst a Recurring Dream*
Yes, permit me to take an everlasting profession
and show your person that my thoughts upon your gracious eloquence
are always of the utmost accepted perfections
which require no further explanation to be redeemed a phenomenal innocence.

For if nightly queries would yet design my wants and needs
please do comprehend that the length of my sojourn for your every part so kind
explains all that is above and beyond a momentary earthly devotion
which is treasured sweetly by the inextricable ambitions of your every goal so secret.

Ψ | mere observations

Grace at Your Table

Permit me to drink your wine
for this I have become ready, willing and able.
Permit me to sit and dine
at the beautifully prepared setting of your table.

I insatiably wait yet patiently anticipate you
like a thirsty person who longs to have their desire satisfied.
I palatably taste yet silently contemplate you
like a hungry person who yearns to have their appetite gratified.

mere observations | Ψ

Just

α *A Convincing Splendor:*
Above perfection
and beyond flawlessness,
shrouded within it's mystery
there always remains something about you.

Yes, I do need to adore you,
for I do want to desire you.
It may be I will never meet you
yet understand how I do wish to surely know you.

Ω *An Evincing Grandeur:*
Above deception
and beyond lawlessness,
clouded thru-out it's secrecy
there always explains one thing about you:

Yes, I do need to explore you,
for I do want to admire you.
It may be I will never greet you
yet comprehend why I do hope to purely show you.

Ψ | mere observations

One Two Another

α Amidst a Parade of Dreams:
When the ceiling has become the floor
permit your Love True to put my fears to rest.
Yet while sadness keeps with my company
do not let me drown within the depths of my own shallowness.

For just to behold the mere happenstance
of all that it means to glance upon the essence of your symmetry,
all that constitutes the mission of my being
imagines what it must be like to warm the very heart of another.

Ω Amidst a Charade of Schemes:
When the window has become the door
permit your Life New to put my fears to test.
Yet while madness sleeps with my truancy
do not let me frown thru-out the breadths of my own loneliness.

For just to unfold the mere circumstance
of all that it seems to chance upon the presence of your mystery,
all that institutes the vision of my seeing
examines what it must be like to form the every part of another.

Parallel

α *Compelled by a Metaphysical Notion:*
Although the tapestries of a thread's loveliness
may factually be working behind the pictures of the scenes
amidst the shifting shadows of the crescent moon
understand your inspiration fills more than just an empty space.

For when the enemy seems to be afraid of me
as I behold the things which do rearrange and never stay the same
amidst the exceptional flower of your undying youth
I desire to meditate upon all that is the future of your personal history.

Ω *Impelled by a Super Mystical Motion:*
Although the masteries of a web's loneliness
may actually be lurking in the front structures of the schemes
amidst the drifting sorrows of the present noon
comprehend your admiration stills more that just a lonely place.

For when the misery deems to be the end of me
as I unfold the things which re-estrange and never play the game
amidst the phenomenal power of your unlying truth
I aspire to contemplate upon all that is the nature of your spiritual mystery.

Ψ | mere observations

Persons Being

α *A Perfected Thought Beholding*
If the words and deeds of your person have presently come undone
please do not ever think that your precious being is to be the only one.
Understand my person is definitely here for your examination
and that the intention of it's honest being is to never bring your existence down.

For while your mystical person does look for it's purest motivation
comprehend my being synonymously beholds thoughts of your elegant perfections.
Realize that your beautiful person caresses my being's foremost inspiration
which desires no further definition to be esteemed by the deepest factuality.

Ω *A Respected Thought Unfolding:*
If the wants and needs of your person have absently undone
please do not ever feel that your gracious being is to be the lonely one.
Understand my person is infinitely there for your imagination
and that the ambition of it's modest being is to never make your persistence frown.

For while your physical person does search for it's surest captivation
comprehend my being anonymously unfolds thoughts of your excellent dimensions.
Recognize that your wonderful person possesses my being's utmost admiration
which requires no further explanation to be redeemed by the highest actuality.

mere observations | Ψ

Post Mortem for You

α *Falling Awake:*
Yes, inspired by my sure lack of it thereof
I do wonder if your very heart will ever understand completely.
Because all of my life is continually for you my love,
I do imagine what it would be like to behold all that is you so sweetly.

Yet, amidst the lurking mirage within this dream
why is it that my being becomes needed by it's post mortem premeditation?
For it is in fact here that I find myself readily to esteem
what my person has been wanted by thru-out it's
over-analyzed under-estimation.

Ω *Rising Asleep:*
Yes, admired by my pure lack of it thereof
I do ponder if your every part will ever comprehend discreetly.
Because all of my life is perpetually for you my love,
I do examine what it would be like to unfold all that is you so neatly.

Yet, amidst the working collage within this theme
how is it that my being becomes greeted by it's post mortem predestination?
For it is intact there that I lose myself easily to redeem
what my person has been haunted by thru-out it's
over-dramatized under-calculation.

Ψ | mere observations

Questions for You

α

My beloved, I just want to know
could I fall in love true with all that is you?
Because my sweet, I just need to show
that I am so in love true with all that is you.

For to appreciate the soul of your beauty
is to wondrously adore symmetry within all of it's forms.
For what else should there be to understand?
Except each gracious day which has overcome strife to be close to you.

Ω

My beloved, I just want to know
could I rise in love true with all that is you.
Because my sweet, I just need to show
that I am so in love true with all that is you.

For to appropriate the goal of your duty
is to splendrously explore mystery thru-out all of it's norms.
For what else would there be to comprehend?
Except each precious way which has undergone life to be next to you.

mere observations | Ψ

Spirit Level I
The Name of Inspiration

α

Yes, I am always looking for the precious one
while I am ever searching for the wondrous one.
Understand this fictional being is always destroyed
whenever my physical being is amidst the presence of you.

My dearest, if nothing is what it should seem,
then comprehend how this actual person feels about you:
for evensong thoughts about you are always silently storming
within the unfathomable depths of the very heart of all that is my mind.

Ω

Yes, I am always longing for the gracious one
while I am ever yearning for the splendrous one.
Understand this mythical being is always employed
wherever my mystical being is amidst the absence of you.

My nearest, if nothing is what it could deem,
then comprehend why this factual person thinks about you:
till morning dawn thoughts about you are always quietly forming
thru out the indiscernible heights of the every part of all that is my kind.

Spirit Level II
The Name of Admiration

α

Amidst the spectrum of the eastern clarion
understand I purely behold the loveliness of your very heart,
just like when the diamond rising of the sun
cascades it's length of light upon the plain of all that is my starlit sky.

As I look for you…what shall my fictional person do?
While I search for you…what shall my physical person say?
Except the things of love which have overcome strife to be true
when the blessed existence of all that is morning dawn recreates the day.

Ω

Amidst the sanctum of the western horizon
comprehend I surely unfold the loneliness of your every part,
just like when the sapphire setting of the sun
parades it's strength of night upon the plain of all that is my moonlit sigh.

As I long for you…what shall my mythical person do?
While I yearn for you…what shall my mythical person say?
Except the things of love which have undergone life to be new
when the sacred persistence of all that is evensong mediates the way.

Spirit Level III
The Name of Aspiration

α

My dearest, there is never a need for you
to purely give my person a concise explanation,
for all that your being has preciously thought
mine understands to be the reason for it's only concern.

Although the very heart of my soul may in fact be
thunderously storming within the sight of it's enlightenment,
comprehend that amidst the darkest of all blinding night
I behold the spirit of your mind thru-out the antiquity of it's dreaming.

Ω

My nearest, there is never a want for you
to surely love my person by precise definition,
for all that your being has graciously sought
mine understands to be the purpose for it's lonely sojourn.

Although the every part of my whole may intact be
wondrously forming within the might of it's enbrightenment,
comprehend that amidst the brightest of all blinding light
I unfold the secret of your kind thru-out the futurity of it's meaning.

Spirit Level IV
The Name of Captivation

α
Yes, amidst this their flawless arrangement
my words and deeds have overcome an inconsequential fate,
for my dreams, which are being perpetually esteemed,
have also come forth so strong to belong unto all that is you.

Yet just to momentarily understand barely
all that preciously enraptures me with the wondrous question of you
and I am bestilled amidst the very heart of my mind
by an answer, which for all eternity, shall never be surely required.

Ω
Yes, amidst this their faultless estrangement
my wants and needs have undergone an unconditional state,
for my themes, which are being continually redeemed,
have also gone forth to yearn to discern so true all that is you.

Yet just to temporarily comprehend rarely
all that graciously enraptures me by the splendrous mention of you
and I am fulfilled amidst the every part of my kind
with a query, which for all eternity, shall always be purely admired.

mere observations | Ψ

Spirit Level V
The Name of Motivation

α
Yes, a sigh of the surest relief
amidst the eyes of the sweetest true,
my dearest, why do I think about missing you?
Please realize what this devotion shall always entail.

Beloved, together within these my dreams,
please do understand I desire more than they do esteem.
For I do want the very heart of all that is your soul wondrously
and the eternity of the very spirit which is your mind preciously.

Ω
Yes, a cry of the purest belief
amidst the eyes of deepest blue,
my nearest, how do I feel about kissing you?
Please recognize that this emotion shall always prevail.

Beloved, forever thru-out these my themes,
please comprehend I require less than they do redeem.
For I do need the every part of all that is your whole splendrously
and the eternity of the every secret which is your kind graciously.

Spirit Level VI
The Name of Fascination

α

Beloved, a sincere devotion for you
penetrates the very heart of all that is my mind
while it's honest conception about you
permeates the very soul of all that is my spirit.

Precious thoughts upon the metaphysical essence
of your non fictional person so concealing
all my being has overcome to perpetually be
what is the exceptional communication of their sweetest feeling.

Ω

Beloved, a secure emotion for you
saturates the every part of all that is my kind
while it's modest perception about you
infiltrates the every goal of all that is my secret.

Gracious thoughts upon the super-mystical presence
of your non-mythical person so revealing
all my being has undergone to continually be
what is the phenomenal manifestation of their deepest sealing.

Spirit Level VII
The Name of Explanation

α
Amidst many a manufactured emotion
please understand my very heart is so thankful for you,
for your transcendent eyes are like ice on fire
when they do pierce the perplexity of all that is the mind of my spirit.

Amidst plenty a numerous fabrication
please comprehend I do deeply esteem all I think about you,
for I wish your being could also behold this conception
because your flawlessness remains the first person that is able to do as such.

Ω
Amidst many a super-structured devotion
please understand my every part is so grateful for you,
for your resplendent sighs are my one desire
when they do peace the anxiety of all that is the kind of my secret.

Amidst plenty a various imitation
please comprehend I do highly redeem all I feel about you,
for I hope your being would also unfold this perception
because your faultlessness explains the last person that is able to do as much.

Spirit Level VIII
The Name of Definition

α

How is it that you do soothe my soul
with such a grace that is so indescribable?
Discovered and then preciously revealed
your mystery is placed within the presence of my secret.

It is indeed a viceless pleasure to know you,
unfathomable are the depths of your very heart and mind;
for you understand the riddle invention of each possibility
which is encaptured thru-out all that is it's farthest distance combined.

Ω

Why is it that you do make me whole
with such a joy that is so inexpressible?
Uncovered and again graciously concealed
your secrecy is laced within the essence of my spirit.

It is in fact a priceless treasure to show you,
incomparable are the heights of your every part so kind;
for you comprehend the middle intention of each probability
which is enraptured thru-out all that is it's closest instance entwined.

mere observations | Ψ

Spirit Level IX
The Name of Declaration

α

Yes, as I watch for you from afar
the very heart of my mind so chose to eternally love you,
just like a planted seed
a sown way of life destroyed turned into something true.

A factuality so verified
by the surest mould of your person's irreducible factor,
for then the soul of your spirit concealed
disclosed within me the sweetest knowledge of your existence.

Ω

Yes, as I wished for you upon a star
the every part of my kind so rose to eternally live you,
just like a wanted need
a known day of strife employed burned something new.

An actuality so rarified
by the purest gold of your being's common denominator,
for then the goal of your secret revealed
enclosed thru-out me the deepest wisdom of your excellence,

Spirit Level X
The Name of Exploration

α

Yes, truly there is just something about you,
a transcendence no other person can surely define.
Every way within your being is so true,
the beautiful joy inside my heart I cannot contain.

Yes, I am encaptured by the ultimate conception of you,
certainly astounded by the truth that flows from your lovely lips,
for it's purity is never corrupted by the deceit of our blue earth;
permit the spirit of my mind to enter amidst the riddle of your flawlessness.

Ω

Yes, truly there is just something around you,
a resplendence that no other person can purely refine.
Every day thru-out your being is so new,
the wonderful joy beside my every part I cannot explain.

Yes, I am enraptured by the absolute perception of you,
verily surrounded by the faith that ebbs to your finger tips,
for it's surety is not interrupted by the conceit of our self-worth;
permit the body of my kind to center amidst the middles of your faultlessness.

Yes.

mere observations | Ψ

Spirit Level XI
The Name of Demonstration

α

Early morning light sparkling
I am so thankful your love is life within me.
No true word can express my dearest
what you do mean to the soul of my very heart.

Amidst such a beautiful transcendence
the riddle of the rising sun tells you my emotion.
Only dawn can define the gracious presence
of the regenerating reality that you give my very spirit.

Ω

Early evening night twinkling
I am so grateful that your life is love thru-out me.
No good deed can confess my nearest
what you do mean to the whole of my every part.

Amidst such a wonderful resplendence
the middle of the setting sun shows you my devotion.
Only dusk can refine the precious essence
of the invigorating vitality that you grace my every secret.

Ψ | mere observations

Spirit Level XII
The Name of Realization

α

Understand I am here for you,
your concerns are so my first priority.
Many believe they are the victims of circumstance
but I know you see that decision rules the majority.

While I do awake each day and pray for you,
silence teaches me to be mindful of the factuality
that we do possess our own flaws being human nature
but this does not excuse us from our own responsibility.

Ω

Comprehend I am there for you,
what concerns you is never secondary.
Plenty suffer rightly the symptoms of consequence
but I know you see that discipline rules the minority.

While I do partake each way and wait for you,
patience teaches me to be thoughtful of the actuality
that we do possess our when faults seeing human culture
but this does not exclude us from our own accountability.

Superficial Again

α *The Depths of Shallowness:*
Consequently I ask myself
why it is I always do become so uninspired?
A thought seems that I am again caught
within the midst of an uproaring suspended animation.

However, as I surely do question myself
thru-out a time and space so unrequired,
I do find my very heart again confounded
by the web of a deceit weaving it's superficial consideration.

Ω *The Heights of Loneliness:*
Accordingly I task myself
why it is I always do become so undesired?
A thought deems that I am again sought
within the gist of a down pouring transcended meditation.

However, as I purely do answer myself
thru-out a date and place so unadmired,
I do lose my every part again surrounded
by the thread of a conceit seething it's superficial deliberation.

Ψ | mere observations

That Which Transcends

α *A Perfected Thought Beholding:*
Understand that my love true
which has ever waited for you
definitely transcends the integrity
of all that could be the honour of mere chivalry.
Within the surety of these defined lengths
my very heart and mind has meditated for you
amidst the times and spaces that seemed to be
unquestionably of both astounding short and long amounts.

Comprehend that my devotion
which is secretly given by your consent,
adequately transcends the intensity
of all that would be the advantage of mere adoration.
For what here has overcome anxiety
to be the futurity of the ebbing present,
now sustains the dates and places which gather
their deepest inspiration above the ways of what was sorrow's past.

Ω *A Respected Thought Unfolding:*
Understand that my life new
which has never hated for you
infinitely transcends the propensity
of all that could be the valour of mere rivalry.
Thru-out purity of those designed strengths
my every part so kind has mediated for you
amidst the crimes and graces that deemed to be
unanswerably of both confounding weak and strong accounts.

Comprehend that my emotion
which is quietly taken by your assent,
accurately transcends the immensity
of all that would be the privilege of mere exploration.
For what there has undergone perplexity
to be the antiquity for the flowing moment,
then maintains the fates and traces which scatter
their sweetest admiration beyond the days of what was morrow's last.

The Conclusion for Certain

α

While pondering if there is one thing else that is for certain
the conclusion of my very heart was that most things can be so unsure.
For if the echo of your memory is just a figure of my imagination,
why does a morrow's de ja vu continue to fill my emptiness with nothingness?

Exclaiming:
"Surely I would not want to be here
if you were not there so I could behold you.
Please do not go away from me
for I do need your sweet love every day so new."

Ω

While wondering if there is something else that is for certain
the conclusion of my every part was that most things can be so demure.
For if the reverb of your misery is just a fixture of my one machination,
why does a sorrow's impromptu continue to still my happiness with loneliness?

Proclaiming:
"Purely I would not want to be near
if you were not where so I could unfold you.
Please do not go astray from me
for I do need your dear life every way so true."

Ψ | mere observations

The One Who Came and Went Undone

α *Gathering the Sweetest Inspiration:*
Yes, as I searched for your person
while circumnavigating the whole entire universe,
I discovered nothing about you was revealed
but did understand that you will always eternally exist.

Yet I continually explained the emotional one
who knew his time and space had truly come undone,
but still I do thank the man of many sorrows
who knew his life new would eternally set mine free.

Ω *Scattering the Deepest Admiration:*
Yes, as I yearned for your person
while circumcontemplating it's sole entire one-disperse,
I uncovered that everything about you was concealed
but did comprehend that you shall always eternally persist.

Yet I perpetually remained the devotional one
who knew his date and place had truly gone undone,
but still I do bless the man of plenty morrows
who knew his love true would eternally let mine Be.

mere observations | Ψ

The Truth Apart

An eye for an eye
and a tooth for a tooth.
A lie for a lie
and a truth for a truth.

α

Yes, while you and I do drift apart
why is it we can no longer ascertain the truth,
the anxieties concerning only one heart
as it's emotional centrality swallows the essence of the other's youth?

Amidst the grandeur of the places you and I have been
why is it the actual unity of these could no longer exist?
It was because the very soul of our mind had taken them for granted,
a selfish effect which caused a dear promise to be an
unconditional inconsequence.

Ω

Yes, while you and I do shift apart,
how is it we can no longer entertain the truth,
the perplexities discerning only one heart.
as it's devotional neutrality sorrows the presence of the other's youth?

Amidst the splendor of the graces you and I have seen
how is it the factual harmony of these could no longer persist?
It was because the very goal of our kind had given them recanted,
a foolish aspect which caused a vow's kiss to be an
inconsequential indifference.

Thoughts of You

α *The Purest Conception:*
Thoughts of you do fill my mind,
yet please do understand my dearest
that the soul of my very heart is never contained
by all that could be defined to be a selfish ambition.

For these notions are the purest inspiration
which defies the working collage of what is logic
but preciously sustains the sincerest contemplation
upon the wondrous beauty of knowing your wants and needs.

Ω *The Surest Perception:*
Thoughts of you do still my kind,
yet please do comprehend my nearest
that the goal of my every part is never explained
by all that could be designed to be a prudish intention.

For those motions are the surest admiration
which unties the lurking mirage of what is magic
but graciously maintains that securest meditation
upon the splendrous duty of showing your words and deeds.

mere observations | Ψ

True Love for You

α *An Intimate Suggestion:*
Yes, time preciously could reveal it,
my love for you within is deeply disclosed.
And if the soul of your very heart and mind would feel it,
please do understand the truth of the thoughts I have proposed.

For these are in fact the surest of propositions
which the essence of an honest person's spirit could ever make.
Not to be confused with the silliness of misconception
because this is a promise that the existence of my being would never break.

Ω *An Intricate Confession:*
Yes, space graciously could conceal it,
my love for you thru-out is sweetly enclosed.
And if the goal of your every part so kind would seal it;
please do comprehend the faith of the thoughts I have composed.

For those are intact the purest composition
which the presence of a modest person's secret could ever take.
Not to be refused by the craziness of misperceptions
because this is a vow's kiss that the consistence of my being would never fake.

Ψ | **mere observations**

Undone No Longer

α Gathering the Sweetest Inspiration:
When so it would seem
ultimately yet indifferently in fact
that there is no longer any reason
to explain the meaning of all that has come undone.

Just to barely understand
the symmetry of your flawless image
and purely I become like the one
whose thoughts, words, and deeds are no longer uninspired.

Ω Scattering the Deepest Admiration:
When so it would deem
absolutely yet inconsequentially intact
there is no longer any season
to sustain the dreaming of all that has gone undone.

Just to rarely comprehend
the poetry of your faultless knowledge
and surely I become like the one
whose thoughts, wants, and needs are no longer undesired.

Under the Sun

α Ante Meridian:
While waking amidst the deepest of every sympathy
as my person meditated upon it's soon to be negated emotion,
the distinct disk of the sun so majestically recharted
it's succession within the diamond-like rising of the eastern clarion.

A Thought Between a Thought:
During daylight beloved do I ever preciously find myself
always thinking about your lovely smile;
a down pour of metaphysical conception explaining nothing else
but how your elegance cascades like a sun shower thru-out a summer breeze.

Ω Post Meridian:
While sleeping amidst the sweetest of every empathy
as my being contemplated upon it's soon to be equated devotion,
the succinct disc of the sun so magnificently departed
it's progression within the sapphire-like setting of the western horizon.

A Dream Between a Dream:
During midnight beloved do I ever graciously lose myself
always dreaming about your lovely style;
an uproar of super-mystical perception sustaining nothing else
but how your excellence parades like a waterfall thru-out a winter freeze.

Untitled for You

α *An Honest Ambition:*

Amidst the grandeur of Love True's gracious days
I have actually wondered within a thought's word and deed
whether the spirit of your very mind will sincerely disclose
thru-out me all that the soul of your very heart dreams to reveal.

For while the essence of my being does eternally desire
all of the Love True which your person has to give,
permit me to display the foremost honesty of an esteemed ambition
which has discovered the deepest recesses to what had been a lost treasure.

Ω *A Modest Intention:*

Amidst the splendor of Life New's precious ways
I have factually pondered within a thought's want and need
whether the secret of your every kind will securely enclose
thru-out me all that the goal of your every part means to conceal.

For while the presence of my being does eternally require
all of the Life New which your person has to live,
permit me to convey the utmost modesty of a redeemed intention
which has recovered the sweetest accesses to what had been a past pleasure.

mere observations | Ψ

With You

α

Amidst the very heart of my soul
so mixed with the very mind of my spirit,
I possess a hunger that only you can satisfy;
a yearning thirst for all that is your majesty.

Whenever by your presence I am encaptured,
your diligence talks with much seasoned dignity,
for you speak with such gracious eloquence,
with these words your existence beautifully surrounds me.

Ω

Amidst the every part of my whole
so fixed with every find of my secret,
I caress a desire that only you can gratify;
a longing taste for all that is your majesty.

Wherever by your essence I am enraptured,
your persistence walks with much reasoned mystery,
for you do teach with such precious elegance,
with these deeds your excellence wonderfully astounds me.

I do love you more than life itself,
for how could there be anyone else?

Ψ | mere observations

Eaves Dropping Upon Adam's Apple

Enter: Sir Lexicon
Sitting under a tree in the Garden of Eden.
Contemplating the universe, pondering eternity.

You are indeed the choicest of fruit from the branches' vine;
so luscious is this knowledge, it is so very sweet unto my spirit's taste.
Beautifully intoxicating like the true essence of a vintage wine
that to soberly arrive at the meaning of this ancient wisdom, I made haste.

Yet as this ever elusive definition continued to play hide and seek,
I found myself counting your mind's conceptions of all that is known to be you.
For as that all inclusive explanation rendered me unable to speak,
I lost myself amounting your heart's perceptions of all that is shown to be true.

You are in fact the fairest amongst all I have ever seen;
so precious is this truth, it so very pure unto the eyes of my soul's vision.
Wonderfully illuminating as the stars where I have ever been
that to overtly depart again upon this journey is my being's one and only mission.

Yet as I prepared to endeavor upon this sweet everlasting travel,
I came unto the conclusion that nothing else truly mattered except this eternity.
For as I compared this 'Forever' to all that I could possibly marvel
I went with the recognition that everything that is you would accept me eternally.

Exit: Sir Lexicon
Disappearing, transcending the physical.

Enter: Adam and Eve
Walking in the cool shade of the day;
together, hand in one another's hand.

Sir Lexicon of Dei Versatile Ink

mere observations | Ψ

Immortal Continuum

Enter: Sir Lexicon
Contemplating mortality and the end of the age of all things.
Understanding that such beauty shall last thru-out eternity.

And if I were to expire tonight
surely I would tell you early in the morning
yet show you purely before the late afternoon
it is indeed your person whom the unity of my heart and soul does love.

For as I journeyed beyond twilight
truly I would remember thoughts of you in the evening
all of the forget-me-nots of sweet moments spent under the moon,
the sacred memory of your beauty as my spirit and mind ascent to God above.

And if Time were to permit itself
then I would speak of all the things you do mean to me.
Again if Space were to commit it's wealth
that I would demonstrate you are more than just a dream to me.

For I do wish to be by your side
to define the perimeters unbound: the height and depth of all that shall Be.
For within you I desire to confide
to refine the parameters unfound: the length and breadth of all that will Be.

Exit: Sir Lexicon
Meditating the moment when all things shall be made true.
Comprehending this instant is the only thing that matters.